WHY I LOVE OFFICER MAX
by Geo Calhoun
(with help from Mommy)

1. He has big shoulders.

2. He has a walkie-talkie.

3. He likes purple paint.

4. He gets rid of bad guys.

5. ~~☆☆~~ He makes Mommy smile.

Please address questions and book requests to: Silhouette Reader Service
U.S.: 3010 Walden Ave., P.O. Box 1325, Buffalo, NY 14269
Canadian: P.O. Box 609, Fort Erie, Ont. L2A 5X3

INDIANA

LASS SMALL

Intrusive Man

Silhouette Books

Published by Silhouette Books

America's Publisher of Contemporary Romance

SILHOUETTE BOOKS
300 East 42nd St.,
New York, N.Y. 10017

ISBN 0-373-47164-5

INTRUSIVE MAN

Copyright © 1987 by Lass Small

This edition published by arrangement with Harlequin Books S.A.

® and TM are trademarks of Harlequin Books S.A., used under license.
Trademarks indicated with ® are registered in the United States Patent and
Trademark Office, the Canadian Trade Marks Office and in other countries.

Printed in U.S.A.

Dear Reader,

Intrusive Man was very satisfying to write. I used our youngest, tag-along son as a model for Geo. It was he who "smoked" twigs, who was so curious, and who would look around with such satisfaction.

And it was he who said his daddy had a "big 'un." To keep from laughing, my husband bit his lower lip, but his eyes spilled with hilarity.

The book came out in 1987, so it was written in 1986. In that time, things were continuing to slowly change for women. Women have had a tough time because they are vulnerable, and responsible for ordering their lives.

I admire them all.

With my love,

Lass

**To my sister,
Dorothy Gittinger Hobart**

One

South of Byford, Indiana, was one of the sprawling shopping centers that had first bloomed in the Midwest. It consisted of separate stores strung together by a continuous covered walk, surrounded by free parking spaces. A shopper still had to exit one store in order to enter another, but it was more convenient for the one-store purchase than a shopping mall.

Hannah Calhoun was in a hurry. She'd only needed Spackling compound to mend a plaster wall and, having made her purchase, she came outside. The strong, late-May sunlight made a spun-sugar halo of her short blond hair as she held the door for her almost-three-year-old son. He followed slowly, for he always had to look around. "Hustle up, Geo." She pronounced his name *Gee-oh*.

Geo removed the stubby length of twig from his mouth and said, "Right." He "smoked" twig "cigars" in the mimicry of Mr. Fuller, a neighbor who was enjoying a spell as Geo's idol.

A man dressed anonymously in a blue T-shirt and jeans watched Hannah closely as he came toward her. He was under thirty, six feet tall and very nicely muscled. He moved like an athlete, and the smoothness of his walk had caught Hannah's attention.

He came with purpose toward her. She was used to that, and gave an impatient inner sigh. Even having a kid along didn't deter the more persistent ones. Lifting Geo onto her hip she busily ignored his approach, but the man blocked her way.

"Ma'am, I'm Maxwell T. Simmons. I'm a police officer, and I need some help." His badge and identity card, in an opened folder, covered his big hand.

Hannah read the card carefully, matched the picture with his waiting face and said, "Of

course. I'm a member of the Concerned Citizens
Watch, number 1436. Naturally I'll help.'' He
had dark brown hair and blue-gray eyes. His
brows were straight and a little shaggy. His thick
eyelashes were a surprise on such a man.

"What do you want me to do?" she asked.
Sliding her son down her hip to set him on the
sidewalk, she told the boy, "Stand right there
and don't move." She put the package of Spackling compound next to Geo and stood up before
she looked back at Maxwell T. Simmons to say,
"I'm ready."

He only blinked once before he smiled and
asked, "Where's your car?" She took the keys
from her jeans pocket and started to look around
him to point out the car, but he said, "Don't
point. Just tell me which way. What make and
model?"

"It's a green Chevy station wagon with a
dented left front fender, and the license number
is L 602. And it's registered in this county. Did
someone steal your squad car?"

"No," he replied quite solemnly. "We've
spotted a man we want in a car over on the other
side of the parking area. I need a natural-looking
way to get across this first section of the lot. May
I walk to your car with you and the boy? There's
no danger to you. I'll take care of you."

"Of course. We all have to do our part. Come along, Geo."

She was so earnest and quick. She scooped up the little boy, who accepted all the varying changes in his situation with aplomb, never losing his "cigar" or his calm observation of what was going on about him.

"Which way?" the cop asked.

"Straight over, diagonally east about five rows."

"Perfect. Walk slowly, and talk to me as if I'm your husband. When I leave you, don't look after me. Just go ahead, get into your car and drive away. Okay?"

"Yes, sir." She was businesslike and serious.

They began to walk. He'd changed sides with her, and he moved so that he was somewhat in front of her. "If I tell you to get down, do it."

"Yes."

He figured her for about twenty, maybe twenty-two. But with a kid that age? She looked like sunshine, with that mass of pale yellow curls around her head. Such blue eyes. Nicely built. Just the right height. "Your husband is a lucky man."

"I don't have a husband."

"Oh?"

"Is the man dangerous?"

"Not unless he's trapped, and he doesn't know he's trapped yet. We appreciate your help."

"I know how important it is. Being a member of the CCW, you know."

"You're a good citizen," he commented.

"We try."

He asked, "We?"

"Our neighborhood. We're very organized."

"Good for you."

"We decided we didn't want to be victims. We wanted to control our own neighborhood. Make it safe."

"How are you doing?"

"Since Pete hurt his back, and got a computer, we are formidable."

"How—"

"My car is two cars over, right there." She didn't point, but she did move one elbow.

"Again, thanks. Don't hang around. I'll wait until you drive on out."

"Good luck."

"Got it."

Hannah hated to leave. She was curious to see if the arrest would work out. She was rather aggressive-minded when it came to criminals, and it pleased her to have had a part in a real operation. Her neighborhood's CCW patrols were now dull. The last incident to break the boredom had been a stalled car that had turned out to contain a city official driving under the influence.

Strapped into her seat belt, with Geo standing on the seat just behind her shoulder, Hannah drove out of the parking lot toward home. Home was now in an eight-block-square urban area that was being reclaimed. The houses in that segment of Byford had stood boarded up and abandoned for years. After due process, the city had condemned them, set compensation for the owners, and sold the houses to applicants.

Hannah had lived there for almost two years. The stipulations were that each house had to be improved to specifications within the first year, which she had done, and possession could not be transferred for five years.

Hannah was the youngest of the neighborhood's urban homesteaders, and the only single woman. Most were couples in their late twenties to mid-thirties, professional people who were tired of commuting to the new additions around the city. They had a new appreciation for the convenience of urban living.

Although a few owners were speculators, who knew the value of the houses would skyrocket if the renewal "took," most were true homesteaders who intended to stay. Besides the convenience, there was a sense of satisfaction in reclaiming houses with spacious rooms, houses that had been built carefully with fine materials.

An unexpected sense of neighborliness had developed among them as they had banded together to rid their neighborhood of undesirable intruders, and had formed their Citizens Watch. Almost all the residents now owned citizensband radios. They patrolled on staggered monthly schedules, in pairs, in cars, until they had so discouraged strangers that the patrols were now a deadly bore.

They all knew who lived in every house, and could call and ask that a suspicious character be watched to see where he went and what he did. The alert would be passed on until the person in question was out of their neighborhood. Their system worked so well that the adjoining neighborhood was getting organized. In time, if they worked cooperatively, the whole area could be alerted to intruders.

After meeting Maxwell T. Simmons, Hannah drove by the cleaners to leave the package of mending she'd finished and to gather up a new batch to be done. Almost ninety percent of the alterations at the cleaners were replacing zippers and adjusting hems. Hannah found hems and zippers boring, and chose to do mending instead. She couldn't put too much time into the job, because it would steal from that allotted for study.

She finally drove into her alley and down to her brick garage, which had once been the carriage house. The alleys were now neat and cleared of rubble. Better lighting had been installed, but the cement surface of the alley was cracked and broken. It was hard to patch because there wasn't a firm foundation. Repaving the alleys was far down on the lists of things their association wanted done.

Hannah lifted Geo from the car and let him walk into the house. She carried the Spackling compound and moved at his pace. Hannah carried her son only when it was necessary, when safety was a factor, as it was when crossing a parking lot at the shopping center.

Thinking of the center, she wondered how the arrest had gone. Had Maxwell T. Simmons managed to catch the criminal? He looked as if he could do anything he set himself to do. How strange it had been for her to look up at him and feel such a thrill of excitement, a sweep of sensation that traveled through her body. Just thinking of him, she was surprised to feel the echoes of that same feeling. She had no time for such feelings, and put the errant thoughts from her mind as she patiently held open the door. Geo took a final, all-encompassing look around his territory before he went inside.

The old brick house was enormous. Victorian style, it had wooden porches and "gingerbread"—the wooden lace that decorated such a house. Downstairs were a living room, parlor, dining room, library, study, kitchen and two maids' rooms. There were eight bedrooms on the second floor. Leading from the foyer was a grand staircase. At the back, for the long-ago maids, were dark steep steps that led to the kitchen.

With all that room, Hannah housed two boarders. Miss Amanda Phillips was an elderly lady. She wore long, dark dresses and elegant slipper-type shoes. She was deaf as a post and never spoke but she had good strong teeth. Her family had been one of the first to respond to Hannah's advertisement for boarders, because they couldn't get along with Amanda Phillips. Sometimes strangers get along better together than relatives do.

After she moved in, Hannah had discovered that Miss Phillips was almost blind. The old lady was proud, spirited and stubborn. She had difficulty admitting to any weakness. At Hannah's insistence, Miss Phillips had recently had the cataract operations. Her second eye was clearing and, with new bifocals, she could see again. She looked around at everything in some wonder.

Her vision had been blurred for so.long that her family had accepted it as a part of aging. Now everything caught Miss Phillips's eyes, so that she turned her head in birdlike ways in order to stare. She was like a bird. She ate like one; she was hollow, silent, and idle. She kept her hands twisted together, her back was bent, and her legs never straightened. She'd lived with Hannah for almost two years.

Lillian Treble was Hannah's other boarder. She was a prim, stiff maiden lady who was a computer programmer. She wasn't yet thirty, but she dressed in drab colors and as if she were twenty years older. Lillian was aloof, efficient, neat, orderly and seldom around. She was very isolated, only mildly courteous, and spent her time either at her job or in her room. She viewed Geo with suspicion. He was male.

Hannah felt that neither woman was living a full life. She racked her brain, trying to find something to interest them. A hearing aid was next on the agenda for Miss Phillips, and Hannah was gearing up to try to convince her to submit to an examination, to see if her hearing

problem was one that could be helped. Miss
Phillips resisted any change, and especially re-
sented anyone who might want her to do something. She was placid and quiet when left alone,
but became stubborn, furious and upset if anyone interfered with her. While all people are interesting, some are additionally exasperating.
Hannah wished both women would catch some
of Geo's sense of adventure and involvement.
He could do with a little less.

"Go tell Miss Phillips we're home, Geo.
Please," Hannah added with a smile when he
waited for the word.

He put his "cigar" into his mouth and his
hands behind his back, as his sturdy legs carried
him off through the sparsely furnished lower
floor. He realized Miss Phillips could not hear
and didn't like to be touched. He could understand both of these traits. There were times when
he chose not to hear, and he, too, preferred to
do things himself. To "tell" Miss Phillips that
he and his mother were home, Geo went into the
room where the old lady sat and watched as her
eyes came to him. They exchanged a trucelike
stare, then Geo went on about his own business.

Hannah treated Miss Phillips just as one did
a little baby. As she worked around the house,
she moved Miss Phillips around with her so that

the older woman had something to watch. It went against Hannah's nature to have an old lady sit alone in a room by herself.

She communicated with Miss Phillips as if she were someone who didn't speak the same language but was capable of understanding her. Hannah used gestures.

That day, she showed Miss Phillips the Spackling compound, indicated that she would be working on another room, and helped the old lady move into that room to watch.

"Come along," Hannah said cheerfully, smiling at Miss Phillips.

Miss Phillips didn't hear and didn't smile back. She allowed herself to be moved into the dining room, which was next on the renovation list. The cracks and gouges on the walls had to be patched with Spackling before the room could be painted.

The house had had a new roof first, then plumbing, wiring, and a new gas furnace. The exterior brick had been tuck-pointed and the chimneys cleaned and repaired. All that had taken up most of the insurance money from the car wreck almost four years before. Now—room by room—floors were sanded, walls mended, and woodwork stripped. The work went slowly on, mostly done by hand—and by Hannah.

"Sit here, Miss Phillips, and keep me company." Hannah had the rocking chair ready. Next to the chair was a small table with a fresh glass of water and a variety of magazines. Miss Phillips had not yet touched any of the magazines, but Hannah was confident the time would come, now that Miss Phillips could see. Hannah set the ladder and began to work.

Eventually Geo came in, removed his cigar and said, "Hungry."

Hannah agreed, came down from the ladder, looked around at another small triumph, and went to fix their dinner.

The other boarder, Lillian Treble, arrived exactly on time and shared the evening meal with a minimum of comment. Miss Phillips silently picked at the food on her plate, and Geo offered an occasional, singularly succinct word in courteous comment, causing his mother to smile.

After dinner Lillian disappeared upstairs to her room. Hannah did the dishes and then began her evening routine. She waited until Mr. Fuller, Geo's current hero, strode past. Smoking his evening cigar, he lifted a friendly hand to Geo. One could set a clock by Mr. Fuller's schedule.

Then Hannah bathed Geo and put him to bed, before she helped Miss Phillips to bed. After that she went into her designated, but unrenovated, sewing room and began on the mending she did for the cleaners. That mending had been a godsend all along. From her sewing she made enough to keep the car in repairs and gas.

The CB radio buzzer sounded. It was Pete asking her to watch for a male, dressed in jeans and a T-shirt, walking south on her street. She went to a darkened front window and watched the man go past then called in his progress to Pete.

It wasn't until morning that Hannah saw in the morning paper that Officer Simmons had indeed been a part of the capture of Lewis Turner, a vicious, violent crook. The police were glad to get him back in custody.

A reporter had been at the mall on another assignment, and had taken a picture of Maxwell T. Simmons. The reporter's story was about the citizen who had helped. It was she, Hannah Calhoun, holding her little boy and walking with the policeman, helping in the deception.

At the breakfast table, Lillian Treble said, "Well!" and raised her brows in a noncommittal way as she handed the section of the paper to Hannah.

Miss Phillips didn't look at the paper, and Hannah didn't show it to Geo. Pete called and said bracingly, "Good work!" and several neighbors called, repeating variations of, "I suppose we *should* help them on occasion after all the times they've helped us." Hannah just shrugged. But she now had a good picture of Maxwell Simmons, who made her bones feel funny, even in a black-and-white newspaper print. He'd been looking right at the camera, with his serious evaluation of the area, and she was a little surprised to see his look was much like Geo's.

She taped the picture to the inside of her closet door where she could see it. A part of her asked just why she would do such a silly thing. It was very immature to save a strange man's picture. Really, Hannah. She shrugged that off, too.

Although she now saw Officer Simmons's photo every morning when she opened her closet door, it was almost two weeks—into the first of June—before she actually saw the real man again.

Pete had asked her to attend the organizational meeting of the bordering neighborhood association. "You can tell me all about it tomorrow," Pete told her. Peter was bedbound.

"Why don't you get a chair and a van and do your own errands? I have to get a sitter."

"Bring Geo over here. He can stay up that late, or he can sleep on the floor with the dog."

"How sanitary."

Pete replied blandly, "Dirt is good for a boy." Pete was single.

"In limited amounts and of selected consistency."

"It'll be good for you to get out among our near neighbors."

"They aren't patrolling yet," she reminded him. "I'll probably be mugged."

"You can handle it."

"That sounds like a man who lies in bed all day."

"Cheap shot."

"The doctor says there's no reason—"

"It'll probably take a beautiful woman in distress. Then I'll leap from my bed to save her, and everyone will declare it's a miracle."

"So you're waiting for something dramatic to happen before you walk again?"

"Why not? It'll be miraculous enough if I ever do walk, why not let it be newsworthy, too?"

"Peter! You're a ham!"

"Oh, yes." There was a little silence. More softly he added, "You *know* I—"

"The time will come, Pete. I just hope I'm there to see it."

"If it happens, Hannah, I don't think I could handle an audience at such a time. I'd have trouble enough just handling me."

"Okay. You've worked me just right. I'll go to the meeting. But you really didn't have to pull out all the stops, Peter Hernandez."

"I might give you some cold lemonade when you come by for Geo."

"You sure you want him?"

"If I can't fetch him, Brutus will."

"Tell the beast to remove his teeth before he puts his jaws around my child."

"Mothers! Picky, picky, picky."

"Check."

So she almost hadn't gone. If she could have wiggled out of it, she'd have missed seeing Officer Simmons again in glorious color and in three dimensions. When he walked into the meeting, she sat absolutely still in her chair so that her rioting senses wouldn't cause her to make a fool of herself. Why should she react so vividly? She'd talked to him for less than five minutes two weeks ago. He wouldn't even remember her. If she said, "Well, hello there, Officer Simmons," he'd say nicely, "Hello," but his eyes would be blank and professional. She would probably remind him of some shoplifter he'd nabbed—or a streetwalker. In a T-shirt and jeans? What streetwalker wore a T-shirt and jeans? What *did* streetwalkers wear? She was too sheltered. She didn't even know that.

But at the meeting he looked at her and smiled. "I see you have good counsel," he said to the group. "Hannah Calhoun is here. We're very grateful for her help. Two weeks ago, out at the shopping center south of town, she helped me get across the parking lot to Lewis Turner. We had him surrounded. If I hadn't been able to block that side, he might have escaped us again. It's this kind of help we need from citizens like you.

"Remember that we don't want any of you to actually get involved. But we need your ears and eyes. We want you to call us, but stay in your houses or in your cars. Never carry a weapon. Never follow a suspicious character on foot or alone. Never try to do anything. Radio for help under any circumstances, and we'll be there as soon as we can. Any questions?"

Hannah was still in shock. He'd looked at her. He'd remembered her. He knew her name. He'd said "Hannah Calhoun" as if it was the easiest thing in this world, as if he'd practiced it! And on his tongue, it sounded like another name entirely.

What in God's name was the matter with her? She'd always been in firm control. What was it with her reaction to this stranger? She was basically sound; it had to be environmental. It was her renovating the house. Paint poisoning. Turpentine trauma. She was so imbued with the fumes that her mind was going. Had it affected Geo? Her boarders?

She sat there, her wide eyes glued to his face. He moved and replied naturally, as if he always had to cope with strange, mesmerized females. He probably had a lot of practice coping with women. It was the way he wore that perfectly fitted suit. No, she thought, he'd be just as attractive without anything on at all. Good grief! Police Officer Maxwell T. Simmons naked! What a sight that would be!

Control. Control was the thing. She had to settle down and get control. She closed her eyes to blank out the cause of her delusion.

"Hannah," his voice came to her ears with a soft, insidious allure. "Would you like to comment on that?"

On *what*? Her eyes popped open in horror, and she shook her head vigorously.

He grinned at her, then mercifully went on to someone else.

She had to leave. She had to get out of there. She couldn't possibly leave before the meeting was over. She would have to wait until the first people got up, then she could go. She held her breath for ten more minutes. She couldn't possibly have held her breath that long. She was sure she had, for she couldn't remember anything in her body moving except in erogenous thrills. What had happened to her?

Several people spoke words that didn't penetrate her haze of thrilling sensations. Then Officer Simmons thanked everyone for coming, and added, "Miss Calhoun, may I see you for just a minute before you leave?" And he turned the meeting back to the neighborhood chairman, who said something or other.

People started stirring around her, rising, talking, and some left. Hannah sat there obediently, frozen in place. If she didn't cause a scene, scrambling away, perhaps he might be fooled into believing she was normal.

He came to her and smiled, as if the sun was out. In a perfectly easy way, he asked, "How about going somewhere for coffee?"

Her tongue clacked awkwardly, and she got out the words with such disorganization that she blushed. "I have to go to Pete's to pick up Geo. Pete asked me to come tonight. Pete can't walk. He promised me lemonade. Brutus takes care of Geo. He's a dog." She said it earnestly, as if it all made good sense.

He nodded and replied, "I'll follow you."

Obediently she turned away. Pete might explain the whole situation and solve the problem for her. She went out and got into her station wagon, and Officer Simmons trailed along, herding her, in the scout car. What would he think of her? She'd acted like an idiot.

Now wait! What was she saying? Whatever Officer Simmons thought had nothing to do with Hannah Calhoun. She was a woman, strong and independent. She ran her own life. Officer Simmons's opinion didn't count one iota! In some defiance of the patrol car close behind her, she even went over the speed limit as she drove to Pete's.

And with a very pleased smile, Maxwell T. Simmons followed.

Two

Still followed by Officer Simmons, Hannah drew up to the curb at Pete's house. He lived two blocks over and three down from Hannah. Since everyone in the area was programmed to be alert to what went on, all the neighbors would see her car arrive at Pete's house with a police car right behind her. Pete's phone was probably already ringing.

Officer Simmons was very quick. Before she had the key out of the ignition, he was beside her car and opening her door. "You should drive with your doors locked."

"Well, of course," she replied with kind patience. "With Geo, I do. But I hardly ever lock *my* door. He can't get past me, you see." Maybe he wasn't very bright not to know that.

"What if I hadn't been a friendly?"

"Yes." No argument there. She got out, and since he waited, she locked the door.

"In a wreck, the bolt of the lock acts as an additional safety factor. It would prevent the car door from popping open."

"I'll lock it from now on." She pocketed the keys and moved to the sidewalk.

"Didn't you ever take the defensive driving course?"

He was delaying, walking slowly so that she had to either wait or go off and leave him. She nodded a bit impatiently. "Driver's training."

"It's not the same. The defensive driving course is invaluable. It teaches you to survive. Everyone should take it, it's worth the money."

"I'll do that." She had no intention of doing anything of the sort.

"Did you take your son's safety seat out of the car?"

She was standing beside him on the sidewalk, and she looked up at his stern face. It was a trap. Feeling a little hostile, she replied, "He's not quite three. He's still little enough to stand behind my shoulder, and he's perfectly safe there. I'm buckled in and my shoulder holds him.''

"Come down to Traffic and I'll show you some films of what happened to little kids who were standing behind their parents' shoulders when their cars were wrecked.''

"Point taken.''

"The hospital rents car seats for various size and age kids. You should get one.''

"Yes, sir.''

"Who is Pete?''

"Peter Hernandez.'' Hannah was extremely awkward. "He was a fireman and a staircase gave way under him. To keep him from burning, he was dragged out. His back was hurt. It must have been horrific for them all. Two didn't make it. Pete can't walk. He monitors who comes in and out of the neighborhood, and he schedules the patrols and so on. He's very good and—''

"Married?''

"No. He isn't.''

"Special to...you?''

"A neighbor.''

"Ah.'' Officer Simmons smiled. "Let's go in.''

That was what she'd been waiting to do while he'd been lecturing her on everything he could think about. She lifted her chin, strode up the walk and knocked on the door.

The intercom next to the door asked, "Hannah?"

She lowered her voice and gruffed, "Naw, this is a stick up."

The voice over the speaker spat, "Don't be frivolous. Come on in. The door's open."

Her lips thinned, and she looked impatiently out of the corners of her eyes before she marched across the threshold and held the door for Officer Simmons. What was it tonight with men feeling the need to lecture her?

Officer Simmons had taken off his jacket as he came inside, and was assessing his surroundings, as all men do, but as cops do especially well. He looked up sharply at the sound of a motor. A narrow motorized bed came slowly through the double doors that led from the hall into the back of the house.

Pete was thirty-five, dark haired, and mustached. He lay on his stomach with his arms over the top of the bed. The bed was tilted so that he didn't have to stretch his neck, but not so far that he'd slide down.

The two men looked each other over as they took measure, then Pete put out his hand. "Pete Hernandez."

"Max Simmons." The policeman grinned. "Come to think of it, I've heard about you."

"I have a lot of friends." The brief words conveyed all that meant to Pete.

"What a way to find it out." With the two simple sentences, the men had acknowledged Pete's circumstances.

"You're the cop who trapped Lewis Turner."

"With a little help from Hannah."

She made a sound disclaiming any praise for something so minor, and Officer Simmons smiled.

"Hannah tells me you're the core of the neighborhood Citizens Watch that's winning a lot of attention in the rest of the city. Congratulations."

"It could be a lot better. Know any programmer who wants to volunteer a whole lot of hours?"

Max said, "Sorry."

"With a grid layout," Pete explained, "I could tell at a glance who was where, who was up to no good, who suspicious, and who a neighbor just out for a stroll. We'd use colors—Vs would be male and Xs female."

"You've put a lot of thought into this," Max commented with interest.

"I've had the time," Pete replied.

Hannah asked, "Where's Geo?"

"Come see." In the wide hall, Pete could turn the short, narrow motorized bed, and he went back through the double doors. All the rooms were empty. There were chairs or tables lined closely against the walls, but the rooms were arranged to suit Pete. Geo was on the floor asleep, with his head on Brutus's stomach.

Brutus's head was turned their way and his teeth showed. Even Max stopped dead in his tracks. One never challenges a hostile dog on his home ground.

Pete commented, "Okay, Brute, friends. Release him." He paused, then added, "You can get Geo, Hannah."

Hannah replied, "Yeah." Pete might just as well have said: There's the cliff, go up it.

Pete explained, "If Brutus gets up and comes over here, Geo's head will hit the floor and he'll wake up cranky."

Max asked, "How about me? Can I get the boy?"

"Sure," Pete agreed. "Brute will accept you easily enough—now." He grinned.

It was interesting to see Max approach the dog. He did it casually, talking to the dog before he squatted down, his elbows on his thighs, his hands between his knees. Speaking softly to the sleeping boy, he reached his farthest hand to the boy's head to smooth back the child's hair. The dog watched Max avidly but made no overt move. Max eased the boy up, lifted him smoothly to one arm and stood up. "I'm not sure," he said to Pete, "that it's the smartest thing in the world to have such a chancey dog."

"When a man is laid out, as I am, it's nice to know you have instant backup."

"What if you needed someone and you couldn't release the dog?" Max asked.

"I have a couple of friends the dog accepts. Two neighbors and a couple of station buddies."

"I would hate to have Hannah argue with that dog over her own child."

"He might scare her, but he would never hurt her."

"I'm not convinced." Max sounded stern.

Pete smiled. "Brutus is impressive. Good dog. Come here, boy." The dog went to Pete, looking more like a puppy than the animal that had so recently awed two adults.

Hannah gave her report to Pete. Not much had been done. The group was still just talking. No one wanted to take on a job of the dimensions Pete contributed.

Pete said thoughtfully, "I might do it for them. It would expand my range." He narrowed his eyes. "It might be good to be a central CW base that could keep tabs beyond our boundaries." He frowned and pushed out his lower lip as he considered that. "I'll have to think about it. Don't commit me. Thanks for going tonight, Hannah. I enjoyed having Geo. He's a neat little kid."

"It isn't you he comes to see," she replied with the bluntness of a friend. "It's Brutus. He thinks Brutus is a 'nice doggy.'" With her wordage and the tone, Hannah was sharing the fact that Geo was a poor judge of dogs.

Pete replied, "With Geo, Brute *is* a nice doggy."

Hannah grinned, unconvinced. "Thanks for giving him the treat of being over here. He has crumbs on his face and shirt. Was he in the dog food again?"

"It's good food." Pete was indignant.

She said, "Ugh," and grinned back at Pete. "I've got to go on home, but I'll be talking to you." She turned to see that Max was standing looking down at her son in his arms with such a...*soft* look on his face. Or maybe it wasn't soft; maybe it was just that, with his eyes cast down, she could see his eyelashes. Thick eyelashes on a man always touched her so oddly.

Brutus paced them to the front door and saw

them out. They went quietly. The door automatically locked behind them. Then Max had Hannah unlock the passenger side of her car, and he simply got in! In a hushed voice she asked, "What about your car?"

He whispered, "It'll wait for me."

"Everyone in our association will think Pete's having problems, and they'll all be so curious."

"He didn't appear sleepy. He'll have some good visits."

She drove, nervously aware of him in her car. He said the lights in the alley were good, but he didn't like her isolated garage. He said, "When you come into your garage at night, be sure your car doors are locked until you know no one else is around."

"We were told that."

"Your door isn't locked."

"Well, you're here with me. Who's going to be dumb enough to attack me when I have police escort?"

"Pay attention and keep your doors locked."

"Yes, sir."

He saw everything. Carrying the sleeping Geo, Max commented in that deep rumble, "Good lighting in the yard. Nice garden. Handrail." He noted in approval as they moved to the back porch. "Deadbolts? Good."

"I had the police do their free house-safety inspection."

She locked the door after him and said, "I'll let you out the front, it's closer to Pete's. Thank you for—"

"I'll carry Geo upstairs."

"No need. I do it all the time."

He smiled. "Let me."

She was uncertain.

He looked around. "So this is where Hannah Calhoun lives."

"It isn't all done," she told him needlessly as she led the way through the sparsely furnished lower floor to the front stairs. "It takes such a lot of time. I'm doing the dining room right now, but I can hardly wait to work on the stairs. Under that black varnish is golden oak! Won't it be beautiful?"

"You've done a lot." He followed her up the stairs.

"Shhh. Miss Treble and Miss Phillips are asleep."

"Who?"

"My boarders."

"Boarders?"

"I need the income for now."

"Smart." He was looking at her differently.

"This is Geo's room."

"Nice. Big. Very nice."

"We don't have much furniture. I guess you noticed that downstairs. My boarders furnish their own rooms. For the rest, I get what we need as we go along." Why was she explaining all that to him? She *never* explained anything personal to anyone. People took her as they found her.

"Very practical." He put Geo's limp little body onto the single bed and began to undress him.

"You know how to undress a child?"

"All police can get anyone out of clothing. We need to know how."

And this policeman would know exactly how to get a woman out of her clothes, but it wouldn't always be done with the efficiency with which he was peeling Geo. He could do it slowly, and it would be mind-stoppingly sensual.

"What's he sleep in?"

"Oh." She went to an old, elaborate dresser. Opening a butter-smooth drawer, she took out pajamas and handed them to Max, who put them on Geo with easy dispatch.

"You might want to wipe the crumbs off his face."

She went out to the hall and down to the bath, returning with a warm, damp cloth. Tenderly she

wiped her son's face. He, too, had thick eyelashes. A precious child. He frowned a little in
his sleep, and his mouth was a little stubborn.
She brushed the crumbs from his bed and settled
him under a light sheet in the heat of the June
night.

As they went back down the stairs to the first
floor, Max said, "I haven't yet had any lemonade, and you promised me some at Pete's."

She laughed rather breathlessly and said,
"Oh, all right. Some lemonade," as if she be-
grudged it.

The breathlessness continued. It must be the
humidity. The weather was heating up for July,
and everyone knew how ghastly July and August
were in the Corn Belt of middle America. Good
only for growing corn.

She fixed them both lemonade, adding mint
from the patch growing in the yard. He leaned
against her kitchen counter and looked around
at the big windows, the fresh curtains, the
wooden cupboards, the round oak table with four
place mats and four chairs and a clay pot of scarlet geraniums.

"Four chairs. What if you have a guest?"

"The other chairs are in the bedrooms and in
the other rooms doing double duty. I got the table at an estate auction. There are seven leaves

for the table to stretch out and twenty chairs! The table was a mess. I had to go through layers of paint on this part. The leaves hadn't been used so they aren't bad at all, but the chairs were awful. I have some in the attic waiting for the time when I can have them repaired by someone who knows what they're doing.''

"My mother likes old things, too.''

"Does she live here in Byford?''

"No. They live in a small town over in Ohio.''

"How did you come to Byford?'' she asked with interest.

"It has a good police department. It was suggested as a place to try when I graduated from Indiana University. Is this your home?''

"No,'' she said. "I'm from Kentucky.''

"How did you get clear up here?''

"There was more opportunity for me here. I'm a student at the business school.''

"Good for you.''

They began to become acquainted. She was excruciatingly aware of him, aware that he was male and that he breathed. Of course he breathed. If he didn't he'd be dead on her floor, and then what would she do? Well, what she meant was that he wasn't a newspaper picture, he was real. Her whole body reacted to him. *Her nipples, her core, her fingers itched for him.* She had never before felt body hunger, and it shocked her.

She stole a peek at him and found he was acting quite normally. What was the *matter* with her? In all her twenty-two years, she'd never been like this, not even with Bernard. Why now? Why with this man whom she'd met so casually and knew so little? If Bernard had lived, would Max have still enticed her body as he did, or, safely married, would she have been immune?

While all that inner turmoil was titillating her senses, her voice apparently responded to him reasonably. They had that glass of lemonade, then another. And finally they heard as Geo thumped to the floor and called, "Mom! Pottie!" Hannah went upstairs to help, and as she put Geo back to bed, she saw that it was after one. How many of the neighbors now knew the cop from the squad car in front of Pete's was still at *her* house?

Max was standing at the bottom of the stairs as she came down. He looked up at her in such a way that he made her excessively aware of herself as a woman. How did he see her? As an unmarried mother and therefore fair game? His eyes said he was interested. In what way did she interest him? Almost shyly, she said, "It's very late."

"I've enjoyed the evening."

He made the house look normal-sized. It had always seemed so enormous to her, so unfilled. She'd thought it was because it wasn't properly furnished. Was it because it lacked a man? "Thank you for helping me get Geo away from Brutus."

"That's some dog. Have you considered getting a dog?"

"No." She stood before him in the foyer, not wanting him to leave. How could she have become so bemused by him so quickly?

"We could go to the pound and look them over."

"I'd bring them all home, and I'm not that fond of dogs."

"Thanks for the lemonade."

"You're welcome."

"I'll be around." He thought that was vague enough and noncommittal.

"Okay."

"Good night." Why had he added that?

"Shall I call Pete to watch over you as you go to your car?" Maxwell was so big and competent that she couldn't resist teasing him.

He grinned. "I'll manage."

She watched him cross her front porch and go down the stairs. The night was quiet, secret, and the air smelled so clean. The stars were out. It would be marvelous to go and walk along with him through the night, to laugh quietly and talk in whispers while everyone else slept. How ridiculous she was. He turned at the front walk and stood looking at her; then he went off silently down the empty street.

She closed the door and turned the deadbolt before she went around switching off the several lights. Then she stood looking out the front window. She would be a fool to fall in love with Maxwell T. Simmons. He was beyond her touch. As an unmarried mother, she would shock his family. They might snub her. He was a man who loved children, and he would want to be friends with his family. She needed to discourage him.

She went upstairs and changed into a nightgown as she prepared for bed. She lay there and willed herself to sleep. But into her mind crept the thought of what it would be like if he was there with her, lying beside her, turning to her, reaching for her with his big square hands. How appalling that she should have such thoughts. He was a stranger!

She was so restless that she went to her sewing room and softly closed the door. She worked on the stack of mending as she reviewed the class tapes. Her goal was to do bookkeeping and billing for small businesses at home. She was diligent and loved the work.

With her boarders and the mending, she made sufficient income to cover expenses but not much extra. Miss Phillips's relatives were especially generous. With the flick of a wrist Hannah could take scandalous advantage of them, they were so grateful to Hannah for taking care of the old lady. In order not to be tempted, Hannah was scrupulous—that was a new vocabulary word for her—and she was very careful to be fair to Miss Phillips's family. They'd insisted on giving Hannah a cost-of-living increase each year. That had touched Hannah's heart, and she'd thanked them. They'd replied, "Frankly, we'd give you double. She's a bear cat."

Hannah had been surprised. "Miss Phillips?"

Twice after that they had given Hannah a Christmas bonus. That would buy her computer. Her busy time was meticulously plotted, so there was no room in her life for a man. He would only upset her apple cart. Maxwell Simmons would do.

When she was tired enough, she went to bed and fell asleep. In the morning she had breakfast ready for her boarders and her son. She got Miss

Phillips up, fed and organized her, then left her alone, settled by a front window in one of the rocking chairs the Phillips family had provided.

On her way to class, Hannah was out the back door before she saw Maxwell Simmons coming through her garage. She inquired, "What are you doing here?"

"Just checking." He smiled. "Good morning, Miss Calhoun. Where are you and Geo going?"

"You know my son," she said to Max. Then she turned to her boy, "Geo, this is Officer Simmons, whom we met at the mall one time. Can you tell him where we're going?" She encouraged Geo, "Where will you be this morning?"

Geo removed his "cigar" and replied seriously, "School."

Hannah elaborated, "Three mornings a week Geo goes to our church nursery school. It puts him with other kids, and the people who are in charge of the kids do a good job. It's free because I trade two Saturday mornings a month there, coping with an absolute maelstrom of children. They're a challenge." She was proud of her explanation. Maelstrom was also a new word for her. She went on, "I could leave him in the business-school nursery, but there's a fee."

"Yet...you have a dishwasher." He saw everything and was pointing out that if she was watching her expenditures, the washer was a luxury.

"The dishwasher is a time saver. I mend clothes for the cleaners. I have a VCR that I watch while I sew. It's very nice!" She grinned. "I get taped movies at the library. My boarders, Miss Phillips and sometimes Lillian Treble, watch the films with me."

As they crossed the yard, Max observed, "Your garden is doing very well. Looks good."

She nodded and asked, "Did you want something specifically? I have to hurry to get to school."

By then, they were in the garage and standing by her car. She tried to open the door before she realized it was still locked from the night before when Max had waited until she'd locked it. She unlocked it, and from the side of the garage Max picked up a toddler's car seat. She looked at the car seat and then at Max.

"I saved you a trip," he explained. "It's rented in your name."

She was silent, torn between being touched that he would do it and annoyed that he had. He installed it, put Geo into it, and explained to the boy the how and whys of the seat. Geo settled himself and looked around. He removed his cigar and said, "Right."

Hannah said a subdued, "Thank you," then drove away, leaving Max standing in the middle of her alley.

Of course, he had been thoughtful in getting the car seat, she reminded herself, but he was too tempting to accept as part of her life. He could distract her from her goals. He was already distracting her.

When he'd taken off his suit coat and loosened his tie there at her house, she'd noticed how his shirt had laid perfectly on his wide shoulders. She knew well-made clothing now, and he'd obviously spent good money for his. So he had money and the gift itself didn't mean anything—except it was a "toe" in her door.

After she'd left Geo at the church, she went on to school. She knew she couldn't accept a gift from him. She should not see Max again, but she needed to repay the seat rental fee. When she was free, she called the hospital and asked about the rental fee for the car seat.

Three

Hannah wondered how she could return the car-seat rental money to Officer Simmons. She couldn't just hand it to him, because she really must not see him again. There is an old southern saying: walk on the track and you'll get hit by the train. That "track" held all the hazards in life from gambling to tempting. She didn't dare tempt herself by walking on his track, so she opened up an etiquette book she'd borrowed from the library and looked up how to return gifts.

The whole thing was a nuisance. She had to

buy suitable stationery and a black pen. She
wrote carefully, declining the gift, then agonized
over how to sign her note. "Sincerely" was used
with friendship. All they had shared was the ap-
prehension of a criminal and the retrieval of a
sleeping child. That wasn't a friendship. Since
she wanted to be more formal, she signed it
"Very truly yours," and enclosed a check.

He was charmed by her careful writing on the
semi-formal notepaper. He read it several times
before folding it neatly and putting it into his
wallet, perfectly understanding her dismissal.
After cashing her check, he went to Farmers
Market and spent that amount on summer flowers. One can purchase a *great* many flowers that
way. Knowing how frugal she was, he collected
odd containers for the bouquets, but he also
bought her a hobnailed milk-glass bowl in which
to place the bouquets.

He arrived on her doorstep the next night, just
before supper, and she was speechless. How can
one turn away a man with an armload of flowers? He smiled, knowing full well he'd trapped
her. Her reluctant words stumbled. "Uh...won't
you...come in?" she said.

He did, knowing and smug, like the Cheshire
cat.

Since she didn't quite know what to do with

him, he walked around her and took his pretty load to the kitchen. There he filled assorted holders with water and stuffed in the bouquets.

Hannah automatically rearranged the flowers while Miss Phillips sat at the supper table, watching silently. Then Hannah set the flowers on the sideboard until she could distribute them throughout the house. There were more than enough.

Geo trudged in, removed his cigar and said, "Flowers."

Max greeted the boy, "Hello, Geo."

"'Lo, Os-if-fer."

"My friends call me Max."

Geo nodded as if that was logical and climbed up on his chair at the table. "Sit down," he said to Max.

That jolted Hannah. After she shot a quelling look at her hospitable son, her gaze rested on Miss Phillips. She had to make an introduction. Let's see, she thought. I should introduce the man to the woman. On the pad by Miss Phillips she wrote, "Officer Maxwell Simmons." Then she said to Max, "Miss Phillips."

Although Miss Phillips looked at the pad, she gave no indication that the name registered and she made no acknowledgement of Max. He smiled at the little old lady and looked into her eyes. His smile widened. She might not actually accept his introduction, but her eyes were aware, and she knew there was a fox in the chicken house. Max's eyes twinkled and danced, as she studied him then looked away in a snub.

Geo said again, "Sit here."

Max fetched one of the dispersed chairs from the living room and brought it to the table. Sitting by Geo, he said conversationally, "I met Brutus the other night."

Geo nodded once and replied, "Nice doggy."

"And very big, with sharp teeth."

Geo removed his "cigar" and bared his own little picket-fence teeth, so Max bared his, as Miss Phillips watched. Hannah faced reality, obviously Max was going to stay. So, she added another package of spaghetti to the pot, fried more hamburger, and added a place for him at the table. Then she took one bouquet, cut the stems to reasonable lengths, settled the flowers into the milk-glass bowl and replaced the table geraniums with Max's bouquet.

As her son entertained their intruder, Hannah chopped more lettuce for the salad and went out to the garden for parsley. She wished the tomatoes and green peppers had ripened, but they wouldn't be ready for a couple of weeks.

She knew the pie she'd planned to last two

meals would disappear because he'd eat it. She felt a shiver go through her. She wasn't afraid of him so why should she shiver? It was anticipation, but she declined to examine what she anticipated.

Lillian Treble arrived punctually and, having freshened herself, came downstairs in her mud-colored shirtwaist. She strode to the kitchen door where she hesitated on the threshold. There was a male present! Not an almost-three-year-old beginning one, but a full-fledged confident, adult one.

Max rose with leisurely male grace and smiled. Geo said to Lillian, "'Lo," then pointed one stubby finger at Max and said to Lillian, "Max." His mother's training in manners must be taking hold.

Lillian almost fled, but Hannah said, "Lillian, may I present Officer Maxwell Simmons? This is Lillian Treble, Max." Then, as per instructions, she identified the visitor. "He's the one who apprehended that dreadful Lewis Turner."

Lillian reasoned that a policeman was a public servant, so she could accept his presence. "How do you do?" She advanced to the table as Max reached to hold her chair. Again she hesitated before sitting regally. Miss Phillips watched.

Geo gave Lillian his angelic smile; Lillian re-

turned a formal nod. It was never too early for
males to be shown their place.

It was a dreadful meal for Hannah. Lillian listened courteously, when she was directly ad-
dressed, and gave a thoughtful yes or no reply.
Miss Phillips, being totally deaf and mute, said
nothing. Geo and Max carried on a running, mu-
tually amusing exchange, and Max replied
nicely to Hannah's comments and praised her
culinary accomplishments—especially the pie.
He loved pie. There went every scrap of the pie.

The dinner conversations at Hannah's house
weren't chatty at the best of times. The lack of
talk now—with a guest—wouldn't have bothered Hannah under ordinary circumstances, but
for some reason she'd wanted an atmosphere of
gracious congeniality.

Hannah kept the writing pad between her and
Miss Phillips to print bits and pieces of their
conversational topics so that, if Miss Phillips
cared a fig, she could keep track of what was
being said. Miss Phillips gave no sign that she
did, but writing the notes was automatic with
Hannah. She didn't know how aware Miss Phillips was of her surroundings for the older
woman gave no clue, except a hard stare now
that she could see better, but no more than that.

For Hannah, the worst thing of all was coping

with Max sitting across from her in her very own kitchen, acting as if he were her welcome guest. There was nowhere she could look—without turning away—that she couldn't see him.

He seemed to fill the room. His breathing, his presence, his maleness boggled her. She could feel her cheeks were flushed and hot cheeks, and, as firmly as she disciplined herself, her body moved minutely in its own strange restlessness. Her fingers would not be still, and she had to concentrate not to breathe harshly. She was very self-conscious.

She must be laboring under a remarkable susceptibility. Why should she react so strongly to this man? None other had affected her like this. It was unnerving. How could she be a victim of man hunger when she had rejected men? Perhaps she *was* a wanton, just as Bernard's family had said. They'd called her "subconsciously enticing." That didn't seem possible when she remembered her one encounter. She'd managed to ward him off all the other times, until he'd simply overwhelmed her. How could that have been her fault? If she'd felt this way about Bernard, she could have accepted at least half of the responsibility, but she'd never in all her life felt this way. Why Officer Maxwell T. Simmons?

She sneaked a peek at him, and he smiled so

kindly at her. He had very nice laugh crinkles at the corners of his eyes. He knew exactly how to handle himself in any situation. How could she possibly know that? To assume such a thing about any man was incredible, but then she'd never seen a man like Maxwell T. Simmons.

After the two boarders left the room, Max helped clean up the kitchen. He lifted Geo out of his chair and handed him the silverware to carry to the dishwasher. Geo felt very important and did it precisely.

Max commented, "That was a great meal. How do you make up your menus?"

"I save the senior citizens' menus from the paper. Lillian takes the morning paper, and Miss Phillips also takes the evening paper."

"That's clever of you—taking the menus that way. I don't believe I've ever had spaghetti with hamburger crumbled into a white sauce over it that way."

"It's easy for the ladies and Geo to eat."

Then Max said, "With all the rooms still vacant upstairs, you could use another boarder." And he smiled.

She was jolted into response. "I have enough."

"I was thinking I might move in."

Sensation swept through Hannah just at the

thought of him being in her kitchen with other people around! What if he were upstairs, at night, and sleeping in a room just down the hall from hers? In an oddly choked voice, she replied, "This is a ladies' house."

"You could use a man. This is still a chancey neighborhood." He was selling the idea. "Women alone are tempting victims. I could be your security." He smiled as if he were harmless.

Hannah's mind told her that his wanting to board there didn't mean he was attracted to her. He was a man alone, and must miss his family over in Ohio. He must hate eating out. He'd relished the home-cooked meal, especially the pie, so he was just lonesome and ill-fed. She was the problem, not Max.

Could she allow him to live with them in that house—and not touch him? She doubted it. The first chance she had, she'd probably "sleep-walk" right into his room and into his bed and... "I'm sorry. None of the other rooms is ready, and anyway, I don't believe Lillian or Miss Phillips would approve a male boarder." She didn't look at him. "It wouldn't take much to get a room ready. I could tidy it up next weekend and get some furniture. You said the ladies furnished their own rooms?"

"Well...but..."

"They'd learn to accept me. I'm really very easy to get along with, and Geo likes me."

"No."

"Yes, he does."

"I mean, no, I don't need another boarder, and they wouldn't, the ladies wouldn't want a man. In the bathroom and all. There's just the one bath upstairs, you see, and they'd be picky about whiskers and—"

"I use an electric razor."

"They'd leave and I'd—"

"I'd pay double," he offered. "I could come in very handy in a lot of ways. I can do all the things men can do." He smiled. "Reaching, opening, lifting and working." He glanced down her. "Plowing and planting."

She choked and coughed.

Quite prosaically he continued, "I noticed your garden. I'm very good with plowing and planting." He gave her an outrageously normal smile and inquired, "Where would you like me to put these flowers?" He waited politely for her to decide.

Her mind buzzed. She had never been so confused. She was a levelheaded woman who'd been alone and coping for almost four years. Why now? It was too late for a residual reaction from the car wreck. It was Maxwell Simmons. He was a wreck of another kind.

She said, "I don't believe living here would do your reputation any good. I'm an unmarried mother. People would gossip."

"Still coping with that label? Hannah Calhoun, you're deliberately reaching out to disgrace. Here you are, a homeowner, solvent by your own work, raising a nice young boy, and you want to wear a scarlet letter? This can't be a house of ill repute in disguise, can it? You're the madam, with Lillian and Miss Phillips as the call girls?" He clutched his shirt.

She bubbled laughter. "Hush!"

"Hush? Here I am a nice young man from the wilds of Ohio in the big city of Byford, Indiana, without kith or kin to protect me, and I'm being *lured* into a house of sin and degradation!"

All she could think of was Miss Phillips and Lillian hearing his talk! Her laughter went into gasping breaths. She raised her hands helplessly to her face, then pressed them against her chest, or pushed back her halo of pale blond curls.

Very pleased with himself, he watched her sparkling eyes and flushed cheeks. She looked delightful. His eyes flicked down her body very quickly. Mother or not, she was an innocent. Did he really want to pursue this? He could be taking a road of no return. He heard himself coax, "If you had another boarder, you could give up mending. Your evenings would be free."

"I like sewing."

"When you begin your business, you'll be very busy. You could have these months to be with Geo more, and to play a little. You've been very dedicated."

"I understand how living in a home and eating prepared meals would attract you, but Max, the ladies would never agree, and this is their home, too. They simply aren't comfortable around men. You have to realize that."

"If I win them over? If I get their consent?"

"It isn't possible." She shook her head gently and smiled only a little in denying something he must want. Her hands were opened out, palms up, to indicate her helplessness. She could understand Max's feelings, for she too needed a home and had created this substitute.

"If I do bring them around, will you take me in?"

She smiled wider. "Give it up. You must be crazy if you think you can convince them. What do we need with a crazy man around here? Think of the...adverse influence you'd have on Geo!"

"Miss Phillips gets away with being silent, and Geo is taking that up already."

Hannah sobered, then said, "Maybe not."

"Notice," he advised. "Lillian is almost rude. Geo has begun to choose when he'll speak, and he's beginning to adopt her superior attitude."

"Good heavens!"

"You need me." He opened his arms wide and smiled, quite pleased with himself.

She couldn't stop a replying smile, but she said, quite honestly, "I don't believe it would be wise for either of us."

"Let me be the judge of that."

"That's like sitting in a tree and saying to a tiger, 'The ground is dangerous,' and under the tree, looking up, the tiger saying, 'Not at all.'"

"Do I remind you of a tiger?"

"No. A tiger's eyes are wide and seemingly lidless. Your eyes are hooded and secretive. Your lashes..." She stopped herself.

"If you didn't use mascara, a man would never see those lashes of yours, unless he got very close."

She raised her eyelashes and looked at him.

"Your eyes are so blue."

"It wouldn't be wise...."

"I'm perfectly harmless! All that I mentioned

was that you have blue eyes. There's nothing illegal about that."

"You know..." Again she couldn't go on.

"This is a good neighborhood for a cop to live in. Not too dangerous; not too tame. I'll have a finger on the pulse. I can eat regularly—I eat vegetables if they're on my plate, but I don't put them there—and I won't have to go to a bar for company. So I'll probably be healthier." He looked bland again. "I'm neat and even-tempered. I don't snore, that I've ever heard. Of course, I sleep through almost anything. I'd be an asset."

"You really wouldn't want to eat what I feed the ladies. You'd want meat—"

"Cooked." He pretended defense.

"That's a step up. But we eat lady food."

"I could have a side dish of steak or chops. I'd buy them, and you'd sear them for me, wouldn't you?"

"Oh, Max."

"Let's just see how things go. It could be we'd both decide against it when we know each other better. We might not rub together well." He gave her another bland look.

She slowly shook her head.

But he smiled and said, "Poor ladies. Miss

Phillips will smile at me, and Miss Lillian will wear a pink dress and loosen her hair.

"You're going to seduce Lillian?" She felt a stab of jealousy!

"Good God, no! There's a limit to what any man will do for bed and board, Hannah Calhoun!"

Again he'd tricked her into laughter.

Watching her, he grinned, then said, "Well, enough of frivolity. I must go back to my bleak and lonely room to plot."

"Now, Max…"

"It'll entertain us both."

He wasn't so stupid as to touch her. Instead, he simply gave her a casual lift of his hand, let himself out, and was gone. Feeling uneasy, she went upstairs. What did she know about him? Why should he be so determined, when he didn't really know anything about her? Or course, she hadn't known anything about either Miss Phillips or Lillian before they'd moved in. They were ladies, so they were no threat to her. He was a threat.

After she put Geo to bed and saw to Miss Phillips, Hannah went to her sewing room and took up the mound of mending. She was so engrossed in her thoughts that she didn't use the TV or the tapes or the VCR. Quite soberly she examined the fact that she was about to become involved, that she should not, and she tried to decide what she ought to do about it. In the silence, she practiced rebuffing Max. She set up scenes in which he coaxed and she was firm. She contrived logical rebuttals, nicely said, the words wisely chosen. Although she was completely absorbed, it was silent, so she instantly heard the CB when Pete called.

Pete told Hannah, "Get to your attic and look down Winston. Report anything you see. Four hoodlums with baseball bats breaking car windows, and they took a swing at Mr. Fuller."

She grabbed the necessary items and ran up the attic stairs. She sat huddled at the window with the CB and binoculars. Although her house was the tallest, she couldn't see a whole lot because it was getting dark and because of the big old trees in their summer leaf.

Mr. Fuller was Geo's cigar-smoking hero. He was a good neighbor.

The voices on the CB were buzzing like bees with reports. "Sue saw them running. She says four. Dark clothes. Running well. Young. Twenties."

It had been so long since anything had happened in the neighborhood that everybody watched and felt belligerent. The police kept saying, "Let us handle it. You might get the wrong ones. Now calm down. If you have any information, tell *us*."

One was Maxwell Simmons. He phoned Hannah and said, "Stay inside."

That made her indignant. "I beg your pardon?"

"I don't want you out of that house."

She replied, "Officer Simmons, you are not my keeper. I'm sure you have other things to do beside harass me."

"Hannah…"

But she'd hung up.

Later he came to her house. She heard something and got out of bed in alarm to look out the front windows, saw a squad car parked in front of her house. Then she heard something in back and went to look, and saw another squad car in her alley. The police were trying all her doors. One was Max.

In some temper, she went down her stairs and opened the door. He came out of the dark so silently that he scared her a little, and his expression was such that a shorter person, who weighed considerably less, just didn't sass. He looked especially formidable in uniform. She reorganized her retort and said, "I appreciate your concern. We are all right."

"You had no idea who was out here. I could have flushed someone from the bushes and he— or *they*—could have been in your house, before you could blink, and locked *me* out! Put a little imagination to that one."

"You're hysterical."

"While four men are running around with baseball bats? Don't try my patience. Pay attention! You are not going to be a victim, do you understand?"

"I'll tell the muggers."

"Don't you sass me."

"No, sir."

"That's better. Go to bed. I'll be around."

She stood there, and so did he. They looked at each other. He said, "Close the door, I want to hear the lock."

Without replying, she gently closed the door, and the lock clicked into place. She stood listening. He didn't move on the porch. It was very strange, with each of them standing on opposite sides of the locked door, fully conscious of the other. It was an odd, intense happening.

Finally, he moved. His step was barely discernible, but she felt his presence leave her. She rested her forehead on the door and felt like crying, but couldn't understand why. Was it because of Maxwell T. Simmons, who stirred such strong emotions in her? Countering emotions of attraction and rejection, of pleasure and dread, of such opposites that she felt torn and unsettled. All she could see in an acquaintance with such a man was complete disaster.

Four

The next day Hannah's routine went on as usual. The neighborhood appeared placid, but it was very alert. Lillian was not deterred by any neighborhood threat, but strode out to work and arrived back on the dot.

Miss Phillips took up binoculars and watched out the windows. Hannah noted that and wondered, since she couldn't speak, what would Miss Phillips do if she saw something?

That evening, Max dragged in just before supper. Although his uniform looked reasonably neat and orderly, he was tired, hot, and a little grouchy. He came to the back door, and Hannah opened it. There wasn't even the invitation to join them for the meal. He assumed he was welcome, like a stray cat that has decided on a home.

Just by the *sheerest* of chances, on her way home that day Hannah had stopped off at a grocery to replenish her supply of hamburger. For some strange reason she had bought a pork chop, a Delmonico and a slab of ham. Not only that, but she'd bought two tomatoes and a cucumber, just as if she'd expected him to show up. And there he was.

Silently, the three women and the child stared at the tired man. Then Hannah told Geo, "Show Max where the downstairs bath is, will you? Please?"

Geo removed his twig and looked up at Max. "'M'on," he said, as he held up one hand and curled all the fingers into the palm several times in a child's version of a beckoning finger. And Max followed.

"Towels on the shelf," Hannah said as he went by her, and he winked at her. The wink sent a swift, sensuous touch through her chest that ran all the way down to her knees, then up her back in goosebumps. She should never have opened the door.

As she set a place for Max at the table, she noticed Miss Phillips was sitting almost straight. Her jaw was thrust forward, her mouth drawn down and her bird's claw fingers clenched into fists! Was she feeling hostile to Max?

If Miss Phillips was that opposed to Max only being there for dinner, she would never agree to his moving into the house. Hannah's instant feeling of despair was something of a shock. Had she been counting on Max moving in and...? How astonishing—and sobering.

She bent her head as she sliced the peaches. Miss Phillips never spoke, and Lillian wasn't chatty anyway, so Hannah too was quiet. Although Miss Phillips couldn't hear, Hannah listened and knew Lillian could hear Max's and Geo's muffled voices, for Geo had companionably stayed with Max.

Hannah didn't hesitate in the choice of the meats; she took the steak from the freezer. It wasn't completely frozen, for it hadn't been there long enough. She put it in a sealed bag in cold water so it would be ready to...sear.

She finished slicing the fresh peaches and put the rolls in the tabletop oven to crisp. Miss Phillips still stared belligerently at the hall doorway where Max would reappear. For the first time since she'd met Miss Phillips, Hannah was glad she couldn't speak. In that mood, she'd probably say something cuttingly rude to their guest.

As she heard the bathroom door open, Hannah put the sliced peaches on the table. They were in individual bowls and decorated with a sprig of fresh mint. There was an under plate and the effect was quite attractive. Max came to the table and said, "Ah..." as he hung his holster on the back of his chair. He was completely unconscious of the impact of the gun on the ladies and Geo.

And Miss Phillips snapped, "Did you find them?"

Shocked, Hannah exclaimed angrily, "You can speak!"

Lillian laughed a perfectly delightful, bubbling laugh that was another shock. Geo liked laughing, so he did, too. But Max simply shook his head.

And Miss Phillips said, "Get them!"

"We will." Max nodded so that Miss Phillips could see his reply.

Hannah was still standing there; so Max was, too. She said, "She can talk! All this time, she could talk!"

Max replied mildly, "It was something she could control."

"She can probably hear, too?"

"No." Max was sure.

"How do you know that?" Hannah demanded, now suspicious and a little irritated for being fooled so long.

"I tested her with a whisper the other night." He smiled with amusement. "Not a flicker." He held Hannah's chair to encourage her to be seated, and she sat down. He walked around the table to his place across from her and continued amiably, "I think she's perfectly capable of faking deafness, but the hearing loss is real." He looked at Hannah, his eyes shadowed by his lashes, his mouth curved in a faint smile. "You anticipate her every need, and you see to it. She hasn't had to talk. You allow Geo more responsibility than you've given Miss Phillips."

Hannah gasped, "I've crippled her!"

"You've entertained her, you've kept her informed, you've provided for her comfort. She's an old harridan. I'll bet she's been a handful all her life. She was raising such hell at her family company, Philcane, Inc., that they voted her off the board. She's been—uncooperative ever since. Her family is amazed she doesn't walk out on you. Did you know they've set up a trust for Geo? Since you only charge the going rate for home care, they must have had a major guilt problem. That was their solution. They are undyingly grateful.''

"How do you know that?" Hannah removed the emptied fruit bowls, put the potato, apple, pea and sausage casserole on the table with a stack of plates. She asked Lillian to serve.

Max replied, "I had to find out if we could do something about her hearing, if she had ever had a hearing aid or a good exam. I dislike walking over people.'' He said that, sitting uninvited at Hannah's table. He took a roll as Hannah carefully passed them. As he broke it and reached for the butter dish, he continued, "Amanda's family is excited over her having an exam, and a little maliciously hilarious over our attempt to get her consent and cooperation.'' Max grinned at Hannah. "They send their love and respect to you and wish you lots of luck.''

By this time Miss Phillips was looking around, watching Max speaking and looking at the blank pad. She bent a commanding stare on Hannah, who was at the stove searing Max's steak. She snapped, "What's he saying?''

Quite blandly, Max spoke as he wrote, "Mr. Fuller wasn't badly hurt. He's fine.''

Hannah turned from the stove in surprise. "Why didn't you tell her that you saw her family?''

"She's rather hostile to them." He smiled at the gross understatement. "If she knows we are plotting together, she'll get her back up."

Miss Phillips rapped her knuckles on the pad, and as he wrote them, Max again spoke the words. "There are several leads. We'll find the four."

Miss Phillips nodded, agreeing with that. It was more response to a note than Hannah had ever had. Max said to Hannah, "Do you need any more proof she's deaf?"

"No." She took the steak from the skillet and put it on a warmed plate before carrying it to Max.

He said, "My God, just what I need!" He smiled up at Hannah, and he was watched by Geo and Lillian.

As they ate, the only sounds were the appreciative ones Max made to his steak. Then Geo offered conversationally, "Max's got a big 'un."

All except Miss Phillips looked at the boy as his words and their meaning soaked in. Hannah stared at her son, then looked quickly at Lillian, whose face was slowly turning scarlet. Max bit his lip to keep from laughing. Having contributed his share to the table talk, Geo resumed his meal.

Max easily rescued the ladies by asking, "Anything unusual in the neighborhood?"

Hannah burst out laughing and Lillian struggled unsuccessfully not to be carried along. With her eyes on her plate, Miss Phillips was unaware of the situation, but Geo willingly joined in the hilarity. Max waited with a patient smile. "Ladies, calm down. I'm not unusual."

Still brimming with laughter, Hannah could finally look at him, and she knew he was wrong. He was very unusual. He was a special man.

Somehow that sliver of embarrassment loosened Lillian, so when Max spoke to her she listened with an open mind. "Do you know Pete Hernandez?" When Lillian shook her head, Max went on, "You should. He has an idea for the monitoring of people loose on the neighborhood streets, but he could use another opinion on how to go about it. Would you give him an ear? I'm going over there, after we clean up the kitchen. Want to go along?"

Lillian asked slowly, "Will you stay there?"

"If you like." His tone was unhurried and undemanding.

Hannah didn't like it. She didn't want Lillian to go with Max to Pete's—or *anywhere*! She didn't look up or speak. Hannah found she was acting exactly like Miss Phillips, and she had no excuse.

After the meal was over, even Lillian helped clear the table. Hannah was brave about it, and even managed a smile as they finished and Max took up his holster. Max and Lillian would be leaving together. Stiffly Hannah said, "Have fun."

Max looked at her, clear-eyed and knowing. He went to her, took her chin in his hand and kissed her mouth as if he'd done it a hundred times. He lifted his head and told the immobilized woman in front of him, "I'll be back."

Her eyes were so wide and her mouth so soft that he kissed her again. Geo stood low to the floor, "smoking" his twig, his hands behind his back as he looked up at them with great interest. Then, like any little boy, he lifted his arms to be picked up. Hannah picked him up, and he sat on her arm, very interested, as they watched Max and Lillian walk through the house and out the front door and drive away.

Hannah turned to see Miss Phillips standing in the doorway watching her intently. Geo wiggled to get down again and went to the front porch for his nightly wave from Mr. Fuller.

Hannah had followed Geo, and lifted her hand

in her own greeting to Mr. Fuller, then sat on
the swing and lifted Geo to her lap.

When Miss Phillips came to the window, it
occurred to Hannah that she never came outside.
She sat quietly behind the lace window curtain.
If you didn't know she was there, you wouldn't
see her.

The summer sun was still an hour or so from
the horizon. Other people came out onto their
porches. They called back and forth across
yards, met on the sidewalks and stood in conversation. Hannah acknowledged their friendly
greetings but didn't join them.

Then Max drove back and, leaving his squad
car, stood on the sidewalk. The neighbors called
to her and gathered around to question him.

Hannah watched and understood that Max
was a man of natural authority. In a group, he
was the one anyone would instinctively go to for
help, and he would give it. He would figure out
whatever was wrong, and he would do his dar-
nedest to fix it. If he failed, it wouldn't be from
lack of trying. In olden times he would have
been one of the warriors. Even in this time, he
was a cop.

Hannah knew he was attracted to her and that
he wanted her, for he'd kissed her in front of
her boarders. He had put his seal on her. She

would be a fool to allow him any liberties. She'd already been through a very rough four years because a man had wanted her. A wanting man could cost a woman a great deal, but she wasn't going to be stupid enough to permit another man to take advantage of her. She needed to be strong and protect herself—her independence, heart and self-pride.

Gradually, Max worked his way through the cluster of her neighbors to come up her walk to the porch steps. Some felt quite free to follow along, and they came up on the porch with him. It amused him. He caught Hannah's glance to share it with her, but her eyes were solemn. He raised his brows just a little in a question, but her glance went to the others as they greeted her.

Hannah saw that Max knew Miss Phillips was witness to the porch scene, but her boarder wouldn't be able to hear it. She must be dying of curiosity. Maybe that was good, because then she might be more willing to have the ear exam.

Near the swing, Max sat on the refurbished wooden banister that circled the porch. The gun in his holster was grim evidence of reality. As he listened to the men who'd followed him up there, he kept one big hand spread on one thigh and his other fisted and resting low on his hip.

Geo slept. Hannah had removed the twig. His

eyelashes lay on his cheeks, and he looked like the child he was. Defenseless. Vulnerable. Each time she looked at Max, his eyes came to her and to her child sleeping in her arms. He wanted her. It was such a strong need that it was like a bond between them.

He knew she was tired. His hands itched to feel the silken softness of her halo of curls. His palm needed to feel the satin of her cheek and to slide down her throat to feel the pulse that throbbed for him. Was it for him? He wished it was his head lying on her soft breast, and his hand so easily curled on her other breast. Then he could turn his head and kiss her there, cup his hand under her breast and lift it to his mouth.

It was then that Lillian returned to the house. She hesitated, then mounted the steps and walked through the group as she went to open the front door. Hannah said, "Lillian, I would like you to meet some of our neighbors."

As they were introduced to her, one said, "We've seen you going back and forth to work. Glad to meet you at last."

Another mentioned, "You work in computers, I've heard."

Lillian noted all of them appeared to know something about her, yet she had known nothing of them. Was Hannah the chatterer? Lillian wondered. She asked, "How did you know that?" and although she smiled politely, she would be answered.

The first said, "My wife sees you leave as the kids catch the bus."

The other replied, "I have a sister who works there. Her name is Karen White."

"Oh, yes. She's very clever."

"That's what she says about you. Except she calls you a 'brain.'"

Lillian smiled at Hannah to make up for thinking she was a gossip. Although she found the people quite pleasant, she excused herself, saying, "Mr. Hernandez has given me an interesting programming problem. I'm curious to get started."

Karen White's brother said, "Yep, a brain."

With the street lights coming on, Hannah rose and said good night. Max went to the door and opened it, taking Geo from Hannah's arms. He, too, said good-night, and followed Hannah into her house.

"You shouldn't have come inside."

"Why not?"

"It was rude of you to leave them out there."

"You want them all upstairs helping put Geo to bed?"

"No. And not you, either."

"I have to. He gave me the biggest boost I've ever had."

"Geo?"

Max grinned wickedly. "Yeah."

Her face pinked charmingly and she scolded, "Men!"

"Ummm. It's very nice being a man. I'm especially glad right now."

She gave him a cautious look as they came to the top of the stairs, but he carried Geo into his room as if he did that every night. Again he undressed the boy. Hannah had gone down the hall for a warm damp cloth and returned to wipe Geo clean enough, for he had been bathed before supper. Then, with the same skill, Max put Geo into his pajamas and rolled him over on his stomach.

"I'm free to give you the same service," he offered willingly.

"Never mind."

"But there's payment due. I've done this twice now and not been paid. You owe me."

"Uh—" She opened her mouth to scoff, but that only made it easier for his kiss.

He put his big hands on her narrow waist and pulled her close to him, then as the kiss went on, his hands moved across her back to pull her tightly to him, and the kiss was like nothing she had ever imagined a kiss could be.

He allowed her to breathe before he took the second payment. As the kiss went on she began making all kinds of emotional little sounds. "What is it?" he asked softly in concern.

"I'd forgotten...how it is...to be held. It's been four years since my parents...since..." Tears sparkled as her voice caught.

"Aw, Hannah, honey." He held her closely, tenderly. Differently. As she wept, he lifted one hand to smooth back her riot of curls, just as he'd longed to do, and he ran his rough palm down her silken cheek and wiped away her tears. "Shhhhh. Aw, honey, I'm here." He allowed his hand to go down over her shoulder, and smiled because her shoulder fit inside his hand so perfectly. But he resisted sliding that hand down over her breast. Now wasn't the time. He couldn't take advantage of her that way. Not this time. Another time, perhaps, but not right then.

However, he could draw her even closer. He moved his hard hands down her slender back and pulled her very close against him. Ahhh. How nice she felt to him—so soft and feminine, so sweetly female. He shuddered with his desire.

Against her stomach she could feel his need, the strong hard evidence of his wanting her. She moved to loosen his hold of her, but he resisted letting her go.

"Hold still."

"We must not," she cautioned.

"Just let me enjoy it for a minute. There's no rush."

"We can't do this."

"Another kiss, and I'll let you go," he promised.

"I don't think that's wise."

"That's what they told Columbus, and look what all he discovered!"

"That old line?" she scoffed. "You ought to be ashamed to use that."

But he'd made her smile. He grinned back and said, "Be nice to me."

"I'm not that stupid."

"All I want is a nice, friendly kiss."

"Sure."

"Scout's honor."

"Well..." She hesitated before she agreed. "A small one."

"Right, as Geo would say."

But the kiss wasn't a small one; it was a lovely, squishy one that curled her toes and straightened her hair. She finally had to struggle for him to release her. She said, "You aren't a novice."

He was indignant. "Of course not! I read how and practiced."

"On who...whom?"

"My closed thumb." He demonstrated, laying his thumb close along the side of his hand. "I would give the crack passionate kisses and press my tongue for entrance."

She laughed. "How thrilling."

"Not very. It tasted like motor oil. That was in the days I was learning all sorts of things. Here, I'll show you." He kissed her again. Lovely. Marvelous. When he raised his head, he asked huskily, "Aren't you glad I practiced?"

What did a woman do with a man like that? She laughed, putting her hands into his hair and shaking his head. He liked that. And she allowed her body to stay glued to his. He put his arms around her and put his head down by hers, closed his eyes and relished her being there in his arms.

There was a slight sound in the darkened hall. Hannah jerked, and Max loosened his arms somewhat. They saw no one, but they'd been reminded that others were around. Geo slept. They went downstairs. Max had a glass of lemonade. He asked, "No beer?"

"No beer."

"I'll bring some. And I owe you for the steak.

That was such a sweet thing to do. You saved my life. And the pie was perfect."

"I froze it last month. I generally make two and freeze one."

"Clever woman." His voice was a caress.

Lillian came downstairs and joined them, quite as if she was welcome. She, too, had lemonade, and she began to question them about Pete. "What happened to him?"

Hannah told Pete's story and added, "He's a classic case of guilt. He lived; they didn't."

"So he could walk?"

"His doctors say yes."

"He's very intelligent."

Hannah nodded and added, "He has a lot of friends."

Max inquired, "What do you think of Brutus?"

Lillian replied, "He's a darling dog."

Max and Hannah exchanged a surprised look.

Lillian went on, "When I first went in, all I saw was teeth. Pete was smiling, and the dog scared me. Pete had me come by him, close." She hesitated. "Then he had me pet the dog while he held my hand. After that, Brutus was like any puppy."

"Puppy," Max and Hannah said in unison.

Lillian nodded in agreement. "A nice dog."

Almost Geo's words.

"Well." She stood up. "I can work another hour or so on Pete's premise. He's...very interesting."

"Very." Max smiled.

"Good night, you two." Lillian went on off.

"You plotted that to get rid of Lillian."

"Right."

"How tricky you are."

"I'm unusual." He contrived to look modest.

"Yes. When do you spring the ear exam on Miss Phillips?"

"Well, there's so much going on, and she's so avidly interested, that I thought I'd let her stew in her curiosity for a while." He smiled like a kind man.

"You know exactly how to handle people. You read them perfectly. How would you handle me?"

Before she could move or object or protest, he had her locked against him and was kissing her silly. Since she wasn't weeping for lost times, he moved his hands as he wanted and ignored her hands scrabbling after his. He did as he chose. Then he set her several whole inches away from him and said, "That way, to begin. I will be glad to give you further instructions in how I'd handle you whenever and however you'd like."

She was incapable of any reply. Her head buzzed and her insides shivered, her nipples tingled, and she was ready for the end of the book.

He inquired, "No comment?"

She held heavy eyelids almost open and tried to form words with a soft and puffy-feeling mouth. Quite sassily, he ruffled her short curls, very pleased with himself, and said, "I do hope you can sleep, buttercup." Then he gave her a very inadequate kiss. "Good night." And he *left*!

How could he do that? How could he get her all stirred up that way and just…leave her there all stirred up? She was ready to chew on the doorjamb or stick her fingernails and toenails into the wall and climb right up it! How could he leave her?

But…what did she want him to do?

She automatically went up to her sewing room and mended other people's clothing—sewing on buttons and repairing rips and split seams.

If Max did seduce her, could she repair her emotions that easily?

Five

In those next days Miss Phillips said very little. How stubborn she was that she could resist speaking. Knowing Miss Phillips was truly deaf, Hannah continued writing the notes, but Miss Phillips still gave no indication that she actually read them. Hannah found she was somewhat irked that the old lady had deliberately not communicated all those months she'd lived there. But Hannah didn't have the time right then to try to understand Miss Phillips's problems, because she had problems of her own.

In all the probables there were in the world,

there was no question in Hannah's mind that
Max was eventually going to get her into some
semblance of a bed. They both knew that. There
was no question. It was only a matter of when.

Hannah spent her days in earnest self-lecture.
The lecture wore new convolutions into her
brain. As she went over and over the problem
of Max, wearing the grooves deeper and deeper,
the lecture became honed and quite succinct.

It began with the fact that she did not owe
Maxwell T. Simmons one thing. Especially not
the risk of another disaster such as the one that
had happened to her four years ago. The lecture
wound up with the fact that she was a strong,
independent woman who could control her own
life.

Well, she could control her *life*—it was her
body that was giving her problems. How could
her body possibly know that it wanted Maxwell
T. Simmons? She had seen and been around
scores of men in the last four years, and not one
had caused her to turn a hair. Max was just like
all the rest. Well, nearly. Actually, he was a superior man.... He was like no man she'd ever
encountered. He was... Now, just wait a minute!
He was only a man!

But what a man! His smile. The way the crinkles deepened at the corners of his eyes when

he was amused. The way he looked at her, as if she were the only woman who had ever looked so good to him. As if he wanted to pick her up and carry her away and do marvelous things with her. Like...

How could her body be so sure? In spite of that one encounter four years ago, she was really very innocent. She didn't know beans about men. Why would she want to do that clumsy, embarrassing act another time just to please him? Why on God's blue earth did she feel the compulsion to please this particular man?

He was so sweet to Geo of course. *All* men are sweet to the children of women they want. Max said he wanted to move into her house. What he really wanted was to climb into her bed. Ah, yes. The very thought made her erogenous zones shimmer and prickle.

She needed more control, for she had a long way to go in the plans she'd made for her life. Soon she would be through with her schooling, then setting up her business, getting the house finished and furnished. She had no time for such a man. He wouldn't be content with an occasional time. He'd want a woman whenever and however...and steak for breakfast, lunch and supper!

And he'd smile that lazy smile at her, with his

eyelashes screening the naughtiness in his smoky eyes. He'd wink at her the way he'd already done, reach out a hand and say, "Come here." Yes. That's what he'd do, all right. And her silly old body would wiggle right on over to him, just like that.

She simply could not get tangled up in an...affair. That was what it'd be: an affair. He probably wasn't a marrying man. He was just nosing around for free loving. If marriage was mentioned he'd run like a jackrabbit. Like quicksilver he'd slide right away and run free.

But before he went, Hannah might get to know what it was like to be with a man she really wanted. When she'd found she was pregnant, her friend Lily Mae had said, "Now you know why I had to marry LeRoy. But it's surely worth it!"

Worth it! It had been awful! Bernard coaxing, insisting, fighting her down. She'd bumped her head, and he'd torn her dress; then he'd pulled her panties off, and his hands had been so rough. She'd cried, and he'd told her to shut up. "Shut up!" Just like that. That night, she'd known that if she ever got away from him, she'd never marry him. And she hadn't. The drunk driver had fixed that. Coming down around that curve so wildly, no lights, and the terrible crash!

Bernard would have gone ahead and tried to marry her when she'd found she was pregnant. But now he was dead and his family had denied Bernard was the father. It was a couple of days past nine months after the wreck that Geo had been born. They said there'd been another man, and she was just trying to smear poor Bernard's good name, with him dead in his grave and unable to defend himself. Another man? She'd been in the hospital for almost two months after the wreck.

Besides the way his family had acted, there were people who wouldn't speak to her in that little town, and even the preacher had made sly remarks. Her mama cried, and her daddy was so sad, pretending she wasn't there—ashamed of her. She missed them. They didn't even answer her letters.

With all that had happened to her, because of a man, did she really want to get involved with another man? Bernard had treated her nicely in public. Would Maxwell turn into a beast if he had her alone? Were the women who liked sex the kind who liked pain? Why was she tempted to risk it with Max? It was beyond reason.

Then, the next morning, Geo came into her room and chortled at catching her still in bed. He climbed up and stood upside down in order to rub the top of his head into her stomach. She squealed, as he did when she did it to him. Laughing, he fell over sideways, as she tumbled him and blew into his stomach. And she knew that, whatever had happened, she was glad she had Geo.

In the days after that, Max would come to Hannah's back door each night in time for supper. He brought groceries with him because he was reluctant to give Hannah money. He didn't want to offend her, but his grocery choices just about made her tear her hair. He bought a *sixteen-pound* ham. Good grief! Where was she supposed to store that much ham?

She consulted her neighbors, and one delightedly traded her a twenty-five pound sack of bread flour for a couple of pounds of ham. That helped. Another said, "I'll give you bottom prices from the bargain grocery, okay?" It suited Hannah. She could still serve ham steaks and even ended up with ham casseroles.

Then he thriftily bought a bushel basket of apples. In June. Last year's, and going fast. She was in a fine temper by the time she'd canned the last of them and put the pile of rotten scraps on her compost heap. The canning had taken all of one precious morning and had put her behind schedule. But that night, when Max came for supper, he viewed the pretty jars of applesauce lined up cooling on the sideboard and beamed, so pleased he'd thought to provide the apples for Hannah. Men!

Then one night, unasked yet again, Max came in the back door in time for supper, and there was a bloody handkerchief around his forehead!

The sight of his blood shocked Hannah speechless. She felt a little faint and leaned back against the counter. Geo and the ladies were at the table, and while the women all simply stared at Max, it was Geo who asked, "Max hurt?"

Max didn't reply, for he was watching Hannah's paled face with some satisfaction. Miss Phillips demanded in her rusty voice, "What happened to you?"

Max went to the table, took the pad and wrote as he said the words, "A baddie didn't want to be caught and we argued."

Miss Phillips did read the pad, for she then asked, "Did he get away?"

Max grinned wolfishly. "No."

He didn't need to write that down for Miss Phillips. She said, "Good for you."

Geo urged his mother, "Max hurt. Mommy fix."

Max turned and looked at the pale Hannah, and inquired, "Hannah fix?"

Her eyes were enormous, as if she were feeling his pain. She said, "Come into the bath," and led the way. He closed the door after them as she turned and looked up at him. "Does it hurt badly?"

Quite earnestly he replied, "Oh, yes."

She made a soft sound as she lifted her hands to his head to remove the handkerchief, but that put her just exactly right to be hugged. He reached out and drew her to him, and kissed her quite thoroughly. Automatically, hungrily, his hands slid around her and his arms hugged her tightly against him, as he backed her against the lavatory.

She gasped, and the kiss deepened. When he let her up for air, she asked with concern, "Were you hurt anywhere else? Are you in pain?"

But he groaned and ran his hands down to her bottom to pull her close to him, so she could feel where he hurt. She stiffened and bowed her back and squirmed, but he only made purring sounds and continued kissing her quite beautifully.

When he let her breathe again, she moved her mouth aside in order to ask, "Are you really hurt? Or is this some clever way to get around me? Is that brown stuff really dried blood?''

He looked indignant. ''Of course I was hurt! Do you think I'd trick you? It had to have two stitches, and...''

''You had stitches?'' It was her turn to be indignant. ''You've already been to the hospital?''

''Yes! And it hurt! They stuck *needles* in me!''

''Then you put that dirty handkerchief back on your he—''

He reached up and untied the cloth. ''They almost threw it away, but there's a bandage under this. See?''

''Why, you fake! You deliberately scared me!''

He smiled. ''Were you scared? For me? Oh, my sweet girl—''

''—and you had it fixed at the hospital!''

''Well, if I'd just come in with a neat little patch on my forehead, would you have gone all pale and concerned?''

''I did not.''

''Oh, yes you did.''

Again she squirmed to get away, saying, ''I have to go put supper on the table. Let me go.''

''You still have to kiss me well. You can't

neglect your duties that way. Geo said you'd fix me." His smile was wicked. "I've been very brave today." He made an effort to smooth away his wicked grin.

She suddenly realized in spite of his apparent lightheartedness, that he'd really been in danger. Although Max was teasing her about it, he'd really been in a fight. She looked at him, her lips softening, and then lifted her mouth to kiss him. As he kissed her, he breathed in rather harshly, in shock over her sweetness. Her lips opened and his tongue met hers. She'd never been a part of such a kiss, and she became a bit dizzy as she clutched at his shoulders.

He urged, "Be sweet to me. Love me."

She gasped, "No." A weak, pitiful word.

"Don't be hard-hearted, Hannah."

She froze, then leaned her head back and looked into his laughing eyes. She scolded, "You could have resisted."

"I've been looking for an opportunity to use that line ever since I met you, but you're the sweetest woman I've ever known. Don't stop now."

"Let go."

"Do I *have* to?"

"Yes." Another hesitant, pitiful word.

With exquisite reluctance, he slowly released

her; and she watched his eyes the entire time he delayed in allowing her freedom. Taking a deep breath which Max watched, Hannah put her hands to her hair and quickly, distractedly, combed it with her fingers as she licked her sensitive lips. Then straightening her skirt, she turned away from him.

He patted her bottom as he said, "I'll take a minute."

Giving him a quick peek, she opened the door and went first back into the kitchen. She had left the kitchen looking frail and pale, but she returned quite pink, with reddened lips and a self-conscious air. She was commendably casual as she served dinner under the observant eyes of Miss Phillips and Lillian.

For that hot June evening, she had a frosty tuna salad for the ladies, with celery and frozen snow peas, potato puffs and a side dish of fruits. There were hot scones with lemon honey, and iced tea. The scones were Scottish and made with biscuit dough, to which she'd added eggs and sugar. She'd glazed the tops with egg white and sprinkled them with sugar before baking. They'd come out a honey brown.

Max came into the kitchen quite naturally and everyone eyed him. Hannah added a baked potato and a steak as his side dishes.

In her growly voice, Miss Phillips observed, "That's quite a...professional-looking bandage."

Unperturbed, Max replied, "Yes," and nodded his head in agreement.

Geo asked, "Okay now?"

Max replied, "Soon." He gave Geo a wink.

That was a perfectly good reply, so why did Hannah feel her face flush yet again? Because she knew what he meant, that's why. There was a long silence. Hannah was uncomfortable. She knew what they'd been doing in the downstairs bath. Max handled himself very well. He had no problem with guilt.

Then Miss Phillips demanded, "Have you caught the men who attacked Fuller?"

Max shook his head.

"Get busy finding those people."

He nodded at her and said, "Yes."

Hannah was a little surprised Miss Phillips was so adamant, and asked, "How did Miss Phillips know Mr. Fuller?"

As Max said, "I don't know," Lillian replied, "I seem to recall they were on a committee together some years ago. They clashed once quite publicly."

Max said, "That figures."

Hannah didn't write down that part of the con-

versation for Miss Phillips, but as the meal pro-
gressed, she did continue her habit of keeping
Miss Phillips informed as to the subjects being
discussed. It was the writing of notes—and having to turn pages—that brought to Hannah's attention how much Max had changed their usually silent evening meal.

Miss Phillips must have watched them, for she
chose a pause in their conversation to ask Max,
"Tell me about your background and family.
Who are you?"

Max smiled with genuine humor. The questions told him exactly what he wanted to know
about Miss Phillips. How many times had he
heard his own family ask those questions about
strangers? He asked for the pad and wrote as he
said the words aloud. "Pioneer Jethro and Pri-
cilla Readings Simmons came down Ohio on
flatboat, 1792. Trappers, farmers, now farming
and businessmen and women. There are Simmonses all over the lower part of the state of
Ohio, and we even spill over into Indiana."

Miss Phillips pierced him with her bird-of-
prey eyes and snapped, "Why did you leave
Ohio?"

"I worked on an original family farm that is
over the Ohio border in Southern Indiana, so I

could qualify for in-state tuition at Indiana University. There're a lot of us."

He'd written, "Worked family farm So IN, in-state tuition to IU. Big families. Exporting this commodity of valuable Simmonses. Infiltrating to save world."

Miss Phillips watched his face as he wrote; with the last three brief sentences, he hadn't spoken. When he finished, he looked at her and they exchanged a long, level, humorous study of one another. It was Miss Phillips who broke eye contact. Then she picked up the page and read aloud what he'd written, and she laughed!

The other two women and Geo stared at this strange, brief incident. Miss Phillips, laughing? Laughing, and her bones didn't rattle! Then, in those microseconds, Geo willingly joined in. It was such a surprise that the others laughed too, gentle, delighted, shared laughter.

They ate their dessert in a pleasant glow of good fellowship, in a closeness that had never happened before in that house. Hannah knew who had changed their lives. This warrior who had come to them.

As they finished, Miss Phillips again spoke, "I will be going to my family over the July Fourth weekend."

Hannah nodded. She had forgotten that Miss

Phillips's relatives insisted she spend the important holidays with them. Miss Phillips never appeared to want to go, but she always did. Hannah wished some of her own kin would ask her back home. None of them had ever replied to her own invitations to visit.

Lillian said, "I've been invited to the lake with friends. I'll be gone all weekend, too."

Hannah smiled at Lillian. It would be the first time she'd been away from the house overnight since she'd moved in almost a year ago. She and Geo would be there all alone. Alone. There would be no one else there! She took a lightning flash of a glance at Max, but he was casually straightening his flatware on his plate. He wasn't a very ardent Lothario, if her being alone for a whole weekend had escaped his conscious thoughts.

In a perfectly ordinary voice, Max said, "Since you will be free that weekend, Hannah, the Police Protection Society will be having their annual picnic with fireworks. Would you and Geo like to go with me?"

So he was aware. She drew a pleased breath to reply, but Geo asked cautiously, "Fire?"

Max replied to the boy, "They're loud and very beautiful. I'll take good care of you."

Geo said, "Right."

Then Hannah said, "Thank you." She meant that for many things.

"I'll bring the food," Max said. Then, as Hannah took in a deep breath to protest, he held up both hands, palms out, and assured her, "Catered."

There were grins among those who could hear, and an excitement curled inside Hannah Calhoun, moving through her body, behind her knees and up her back and licking in her stomach. How strange to feel those delicious sensations. It was a little scary.

Lillian rose from her chair, exclaiming, "Good heavens, look at the time! We've never taken this long at dinner. I'm late; sorry to leave you with the kitchen, Hannah. I'm due at Pete's." At least she'd quit calling him Mr. Hernandez.

Two things amazed Hannah. Lillian had never helped in the kitchen before Max started coming to dinner, and they'd had such a pleasant time at the table that the punctual Lillian had lost track of the hour. She was probably late for the first time in her life. It was all because of Max.

However, even knowing she was late, Lillian went upstairs to her room. When she came down, she'd changed into a cool green cotton dress that did marvelous things to her green eyes. Hannah blinked. Lillian wore grey, black or mud-brown. Lillian in green! How rash! How pretty. And she'd used makeup! Not a whole lot, but since she never wore it, anything was noticeable.

Lillian paused at the door to say, "I may be late, but I have my key. Don't worry about me." Then she left.

Hannah looked at Max. "She had on *lipstick!*"

"The hussy!" His tone was exaggerated in scandal.

Geo tried the word, "Huzzy! Fuzzy?"

Max then told Geo the rhyme about the Fuzzy Wuzzy Bear who wasn't fuzzy, was he? Geo was too young to understand play on words or sounds, but he was very kind about it for he grinned and said, "Right!"

Miss Phillips rose from her seat and said to Hannah quite formally, "Excuse me, I believe I'll read upstairs. Good night, Officer Simmons."

Max had reached automatically to help Amanda Phillips with her chair, so he'd risen. They exchanged another look, and she went on out of the room.

As Max and Hannah straightened the kitchen, he recited the poem about the handsome worm named Ooey Gooey. Geo went into a peal of chortles that made Max grin back. Then his lazy eyes went to Hannah, and he told her, "You've got a nice kid."

They went out to sit on the porch swing, and neighbors drifted over to talk to Max. The neighbors had always been friendly and waved to her, but none had ever before come onto the porch to talk of an evening.

Geo went to sleep on Max's lap, and after a time they took him upstairs to put him to bed. With the days of summer, and Geo playing outside almost all day, he had his bath before supper. It was black-bathwater time, and getting his rosy little body clean was a special pleasure for Hannah.

Max went down to the kitchen to make some lemonade while Hannah helped Miss Phillips get ready for bed. She was still silent with Hannah. What an exasperating old lady! Maybe it wasn't easy to be so old that she had to have someone help her to bed. As usual, Hannah smiled at Miss Phillips and said good-night. As she went through the bedroom door, the rusty old voice replied, "Good night, Hannah. Thank you."

It was the first time Miss Phillips had ever used those words.

Hannah and Max took their lemonade back

out onto the dark porch and again sat in the swing. They were contented there, Max's toe keeping a gentle motion. He put his arm along the back of the swing and turned toward her. "Tell me about Geo's father." This had been gnawing at Max.

Hannah looked at Max for an uncertain minute. Must she tell him? There had to be some sort of explanation. She told the truth, and she said it quickly. "We were engaged. I was just eighteen. He wanted to... But I didn't. He made me. On the way home a drunken driver hit us—" her voice slowed "—and Bernard was killed. I was badly hurt. The doctor saw the bruises and knew. He was careful with the medication...in case I was...pregnant. He knew I'd been engaged, and that he'd, Bernard had, we'd had intercourse." She looked at Max in pain.

He was acutely aware of her words—she had never said it was lovemaking. He asked, "What sort of...bruises?" His face was smooth, his voice normal.

One hand touched her head, then her breasts, as the other hand indicated the top of her thighs.

"Intercourse?" His eyes were slits. "Sounds more like rape."

That was a new interpretation of what had happened. No one had suggested such a term before. She had known Bernard all her life, he'd been after her since she'd turned fifteen, her family said he was a nice boy, and no one else dated her. In that little town, all the other young men considered her Bernard's. They became engaged, and after the wreck, when it was clear she was pregnant, his family said she was a loose woman, inviting it from God only knew who all.

But Bernard had…raped her? She looked up at Max as the realization of exactly what Bernard had done to her came clear. "Yes." All the confused guilt she'd carried all those years rolled off her back. She had believed her parents' shame.

Then she blurted, "The doctor gave me the name of a lawyer who was his friend. They were very kind to me. We sued for the wreck. I had been badly hurt. The lawyer didn't work on contingency—taking a third to a half of the settlement—but worked only on regular time fees, so I got enough to pay my bills, move away from all the scandal, buy this house, and go to school."

"And your family?" His voice was soft.

"They are ashamed of me. I have an illegitimate child, you see."

Max made a harsh sound that was all the more

poignant because it was smothered. He took her into his arms very gently, "What a tough time you've had."

She didn't cry. She'd done all that years ago, but she was almost overwhelmed by his compassion, by his holding her. In all that time, no one had ever just held her to comfort her. It was Max who finally gave that to her.

So they were in the swing, Hannah's feet curled up against Max as she lay in his arms, when Lillian came storming up the walk, up the steps, and onto the porch. She was temporarily startled to see them, and she hesitated. She was furious! "Men!" she said, and stormed into the house.

Hannah stirred in order to look up into Max's face. "What in the world?"

Max laughed low and wickedly. "Maybe Pete isn't as disabled as we thought."

Six

Lillian barely had time to get upstairs before the phone began to ring. The two on the porch smiled at each other. "Pete," they said simultaneously, shaking their heads and letting it ring, waiting to see if Lillian would give in and answer it. She didn't.

The phone rang and rang and rang. There was no one in the house it could disturb. Miss Phillips couldn't hear it. Geo was so tired these nights that he never wakened; and his room was some distance from the upstairs phone. Only Lillian would be disturbed by the insistent ringing. Or would she be pleased?

The CB in the entrance came on, "Fourteen-twenty-two calling fourteen-thirty-six."

"That's Pete calling me. He's worried about Lillian." Hannah started to rise.

Max said, "Let me." He untangled himself from Hannah and put a big pillow in his place for her to lean against as the call came a second time. He went into the hall, and Hannah heard him say drolly, "Hi. Max here. Looking for someone?"

That did eliminate Pete's need to use Lillian's name for the neighbors listening on their CBs with eager ears. He said a terse, "Yeah."

"All's tidy, but there's a foul wind a-blowing across the icy northland."

"Tell me about it."

Max laughed heartlessly. "Max clear."

Instead of being formal in his reply, Peter said, "I wish I was."

The phone was still ringing. Then about four voices on the CB asked variations of, "What's going on out there?"

Pete's disgusted voice replied, "No problem," but the phone kept on ringing. Pete gave up before Lillian did.

Back on the swing, Max was into some serious kissing. He was very pleased to feel Hannah trembling in his arms, her breath shaky, her fingers restless. He would have thought she might be scared of him, but she clutched him and her mouth was eager...before she began to resist.

"Just a few more kisses."

"I have to study."

"Take me in as a boarder. You can stay home and...play house with me."

Yes, play house. That would be all. "I really have to study." Although she'd never faltered in her resolve, she was suddenly more determined than ever that she would finish school.

"I know I can get the ladies to agree to share the house with me. Up until tonight Lillian was just about convinced I was human and tolerable. I think I'll go over and break Pete's nose."

"He has enough problems."

"Speaking of problems, I have a dandy." He tried to coax her back against him.

Heartlessly she repeated, "I really must go in."

"You have your commitments confused. I'm a wounded man. I need tender loving care."

"When you take off that bandage, and you should so the air can get to the wound, how are you going to explain those stitches to Miss Phillips? She's already commented on how professional the bandaging was. She might accept that

I could do a reasonable bandage but stitches will take some explaining.''

"I'm like Walter Mitty, and I always set my own broken bones and stitch my own wounds.'' His voice was grave and his face sober.

She laughed.

"What a hard-hearted woman you are, Hannah, to laugh over my setting my own bones and stitching…''

"Go home.''

"I have no home.'' He looked away to the street forlornly, sighing hugely.

"You're a ham.''

Chattily, he took that up, "I'll never again buy you a sixteen-pound ham! Are we through with it yet?''

"Yes.'' He didn't realize she'd gotten rid of more than two-thirds of it?

"Why don't I get us a side of beef and…''

"*No.*''

That surprised him. "Why not? It's much more economical, buying bulk.''

"No!'' Her voice was a little strident. "I do not want a side of beef!''

"It costs more to buy steaks one at a time.''

"I don't have room to store that much food. And the ladies don't eat that much beef.''

"I do.''

"You may not move in here, Max. And you really shouldn't eat here every day. It doesn't look right."

"With three chaperons? What do you mean it doesn't look right? I'm a perfectly decent man! I'm not going to ruin your reputation. I am..."

Although he continued to talk, Hannah didn't hear anything beyond the words that he couldn't ruin her reputation. That was true. It was already ruined. How could a man like Max do her any more harm? It would be more the other way around.

It was five days until the Fourth of July and the picnic. He was going to take her to the Police Society picnic, and she would meet his friends. But nowadays men were quite bold in taking women around who were temporarily...good friends.

People would think Max was sleeping with her. They'd say, "That Hannah Calhoun has her claws in that nice Max Simmons. Wonder if his family knows about her?"

She was the first of her family to do anything scandalous. All of the people, back in her families, had been honorable—other than the fact that some had made a little moonshine. Only she was an unwed mother. Which made her sound as if she was as immoral and as loose as Bernard's family said she was. She was the first. The first who was caught. Bernard was dead, and she hadn't even dated anyone else. What trickery had put her in such a position?

It was a good thing she'd left town and come north. Back home, the men had thought her fair game. She'd had a tough time convincing them she was not. Her brother had helped her twice, telling men to run along and quit bothering her, but the men had hooted, saying it was Hannah who "bothered" all of them. It was her fault.

One of her sisters flew in a rage when she found Hannah cornered on the street by two men who were talking dirty to her. Hannah was crying and her sister was a fury, swinging her purse and kicking at them. They had laughed, offering to take her instead, and her sister had turned on Hannah. "See?" she cried at Hannah, "You did this to *all* of us!"

The hill people have the reputation for being old-fashioned. But Hannah knew morals were important, and she'd been caught in the black-and-white code of morality. No gray. Although she was the victim of it, she could understand the importance of the code. There must be rules of conduct.

But she was attracted to Max, who was after her. He was from a solid farm family like her

own that had the old values. There was no way
ever his family could approve of her. She should
never see him again. She knew she was too attracted to him. She had never felt so safe as in
his arms there in that house. Perhaps it had just
been too long since anyone had shown her any
affection, and it was the caring she needed, not
sex.

But the next night, just before supper, Max
came in the back door as if he owned the place.
As he went by her, he dropped a brief kiss on
her surprised lips, and greeted everyone in the
kitchen, saying, "The good guys are still
ahead," and went on through to the bath as if
he was home.

How had she allowed that conduct to become
so natural? Why had she set a place for him at
the table? Why had she thawed a pork chop? It
wasn't a half-inch lady one, but one an inch and
a half thick. There it was, grilling under a lid
over slow heat so it would cook through and stay
moist.

There were summer yams and crisp, tart cole-
slaw and some of that applesauce. There was
cornbread and honey, iced tea, milk and a lemon
cake. Hannah had sifted powdered sugar over a
lace cutout so that a design had filtered onto the
cake's top.

He came from the back hall and hung his holster on a peg just inside the hall. He automatically put his gun in the waistband of his trousers at the small of his back, and he smiled at all of them as if they were delighted to see him. Geo said with satisfaction, "Max."

As if that made good sense, Max said with equal satisfaction, "Right, Geo."

Geo chortled as if their conversation was *just* right.

Miss Phillips gave her usual brief glance to show she knew he was there but said nothing. Lillian gave Max a cool look and then went about the business of eating, giving no indication that anyone else was around.

Max, of course, couldn't leave well enough alone. "Pete contact you today?"

Lillian flared her eyes at him.

"You worried him last night, stomping off that way. He had to use the CB to find out if you got home all right."

She didn't move her head, but raised her eyes to glare at him.

"He didn't like it that you were out after dark that way, and you didn't answer the phone."

She put out her chin and snapped, "You two were down on the porch. Why didn't one of you answer it?"

Max smiled, put out his chin exactly as she'd done, and answered back as a brother would, "Because we knew it was for you."

Lillian went, "Haauhh!" in an indignant, no-word ejection of breath for something to reply, and went back to precisely cutting up her lady's half-inch pork chop.

"Uh, Max…" Hannah said, trying for peace.

But Max went on, "You're being mean to poor old Pete. What could he possibly have done to make you so mad at him?"

Eyes flashing, Lillian reared back and snorted. Then she threw down her napkin and stood up. "What did *I* do?" She shoved back her chair and left the table, striding through the other room and storming up the stairs.

Geo watched and mentioned, "Mad."

"Angry," corrected Hannah.

"Yep," agreed Geo.

"Max," Hannah began in a censorious voice.

Miss Phillips was looking at Lillian's half-eaten meal and empty chair. "What was that about?"

Hannah glared at Max, handed him the pad and pencil and said, "*You* tell her!"

Max smiled at Miss Phillips, wrote rapidly, then handed her the pad. She looked at him suspiciously then slowly took the pad and read the words. She looked down, then up at Max in a weighing way. She read the message again, before she put the pad down and continued to eat.

Before dessert was served, Hannah took Lillian's meal upstairs to her with a slice of the lemon cake. "I'm sorry if Max annoyed you."

Lillian was sitting at her front window, which looked out toward the Hernandez house. She turned, stood up, took the tray Hannah carried and set it on a table nearby. "Thank you. You're always so sweet. Miss Phillips and I don't deserve you. I'm sorry to have caused a scene."

"Max is like all men. They stick together. When there's a disagreement between a man and a woman, they just naturally blame the woman. He shouldn't have teased you about it. He was...Lillian, I'm sure he didn't mean to upset you." That was a lie meant to placate her. Max had done it deliberately.

"He really didn't. It's Pete. I just didn't expect... It doesn't matter. I'm sorry I lost my temper. This has been a difficult day. I-I didn't sleep much last night."

"Is there anything I can do?"

"No. No. It's all right. I'm fine." She said that as she paced around her room, wringing her hands. "I overreacted to Pete last night. I really

was a fool. He didn't mean... I don't know...
Oh, I could cry!''

"It does help on occasion," Hannah said rue-
fully, ''but generally it isn't worth the headache.''

Lillian smiled, but she turned and looked out
the window, toward Pete's house.

"You know he's home. Why not go over and
talk to him?''

"I'd be too embarrassed.''

"What's a little embarrassment between
friends?''

"I can't.''

"You're going to shun Pete because you
might be embarrassed?'' Lillian looked at her
and groaned. Hannah was amazed to think Lillian could be emotional, vulnerable, could feel
like a fool. Very softly Hannah said, "He can
only tell you to get lost.''

"Oh, Hannah.''

"Are you better off with, or without?''

"I suppose I could walk over there.'' The
words were dragged out with great reluctance.

"Do it. You're no coward." Hannah said
bracingly, ''I'll put your pork chop in the fridge,
and you can have the cake later.'' She started
away, then turned back to Lillian. "Or you can
take two pieces over to Pete's.''

"Going to Pete's?" Max enquired cheerily from the doorway. "Good. I've got to see him, and you can ride with me." He smiled as if it would be a casual jaunt.

Just what was Max doing upstairs? Hannah drew in a long, indignant breath, ready to lambast him. Then she heard Lillian say, "Why, thank you, Max. That'll be fine."

Max grinned at Hannah as he and Lillian left.

Hannah went downstairs to the table. She picked up the pad and read the explanation Max had written on the pad for Miss Phillips when Lillian had left the table: "If you'll go for the ear exam, they might be able to help you, then you could listen to all that goes on in this house—or at board meetings." But he hadn't written another thing! He hadn't told Miss Phillips anything!

How clever that man was. If he hadn't nudged Lillian into a blowup, she wouldn't have recognized how silly she was being, and wouldn't be on her way to Pete's house. Not only was he manipulating Lillian, but he was goading that poor old lady to get her hearing exam. Wouldn't it be marvelous if she could be helped!

Hannah cleared up the kitchen, then wrote a summary of what was going on before she

sought out Miss Phillips in her room and gave
her the pad to read. The old lady made no pre-
tense about whether or not she read it. She did.
Then she looked up at Hannah, and her wrinkles
creased in a smile as she shook her head.
"Max," she said, and chuckled.

With her ears strained to hear the doorbell,
Hannah went to do her mending. The doors were
locked, of course, with the darkening evening
and while she was upstairs. She sewed with great
efficiency. Geo was around and about, busy with
his various projects, before she put him to bed.
After that she helped Miss Phillips get ready for
the night.

Hannah went back to her sewing and about
jumped out of her skin when she caught a move-
ment out of the corner of her eye. She jerked
her head around to see what it was, and there
stood Max in her locked house! "Where did you
come from?" she demanded. "How did you get
in?"

"Any cop worth his salt can pick a lock."

"I have deadbolts on my doors."

"You didn't put it on the front door tonight,
Hannah. We have to have a very serious talk
about how careless you are."

"No normal person could get inside."

"No normal person tries." He leaned there in

her doorway, watching her, his hands in his trouser pockets. He was a gorgeous man, with a stubborn lower lip, dark unruly hair, and lashes that were wasted on a man. He was weather-tanned, and his shoulders were wide enough to carry all the cares in the world. His eyes rested on her with interest. She, Hannah Calhoun, had this man's attention.

She looked back at him, and her eyes were large and solemn. "What happened?"

"I got in through the front door. No problem. I should have a key."

"No." Her lips stayed in the O position for a count of two as she imagined Max having free access to her house. Then she asked, "Is Lillian all right?"

"As I left, Pete held out a hand to her and she went over and put hers in his. I wanted to stay, but I never butt in on other people's business."

How dare he say such a thing? Having picked a lock to get into her house, he had the *nerve* to stand there quite placidly and say that he didn't butt in on other people's lives! Hannah used full-scale sarcasm as she agreed, "Of course not. You'd never interfere."

"Well, yes, I would, with you. You *have* to pay attention to security, Hannah. Yours isn't

the safest neighborhood in the world. Mind me
in this.''

''Everybody here watches everybody else.''

''I could show you a stack of cases where
things were done under the noses of any number
of people.''

''I will lock the door.''

''I'm having a hell of a time getting you to
shape up, Hannah. Come over here and let me
get started on the rest of you.''

''Max...'' she began cautiously.

''Lillian won't be home for a time. Maybe not
all night. Amanda can't hear, and Geo is out like
a light. I checked. Come here and tell me you're
mad about me and crave my body.''

''Max...''

''Oh, well, come here and let me practice
blindfolded identification of culprits. I'm very
poor on that. I need more practice. The light
isn't always good, and sometimes it's very difficult. Especially now when some men wear earrings in both ears. Earrings used to be a clue,
but these days it just doesn't mean a thing!''

Mesmerized by him, and by her own body's
reaction to him, she breathed, ''I rarely wear earrings.''

''See?'' His voice was low and reedy. ''I'd

have to find another way of figuring you out. Come here. Let me guess. It's good practice."

She got up like Trilby and walked to her Svengali. He didn't move. He just stood there, lounging in the doorway with his hands in his pockets, watching her. His breath was a little quicker, and his eyelashes screened his eyes.

She stood in front of him, and her expression was very serious. Her own breath quickened, and she was extraordinarily conscious of her body, of her breasts, of her thighs. How strange he made her feel.

Very slowly he pulled his hands from his pockets and stood up, planting his big feet as his big hands reached for her waist to pull her to him. He bent his head down and kissed her.

When he lifted his mouth, in the silence of that big house, she asked, "You always kiss suspects first?"

He narrowed his eyes; then his face changed and he said, "It's probably the wrong way to begin."

"You might be slapped." No woman would ever slap Max.

"Or...he might kiss back!"

"There's that."

"You kissed me back."

"Yes."

"Hannah, I want you very badly."

"I know."

"Make love with me."

"I'm...not sure."

"We'll have this weekend together. I'll take good care of you. I'll protect you. Nothing will happen to you, I promise."

"I'll...see." She looked up at him and added, "There's Geo."

"He likes me. He'll accept that I will be with you. He won't mind, I promise."

"I've never been with...anyone, except that once."

"This won't be anything like then. I promise you."

"Oh, Max..." She was very unsure.

"Don't worry about a thing. It'll be fine. I promise you that, Hannah."

He kissed her again in that lovely, lovely way. His hands moved, and she stretched up along him and kissed him back. He thrilled her. If he'd wanted to, he could have taken her to her bed, right then, and she would have let him take her. But he didn't.

He wanted her to be sure, and to come to him with no hesitation. He wanted her to want him, too. Not just to give herself, but to share herself with him. How he longed for her! He lifted his

mouth from her throat and looked into her sweet
face. She was like sunshine to him. Her com-
plexion was the rare perfection some blondes
have, like alabaster flushed softly with pink. She
was beautiful.

Max harbored a great distaste for the clumsy
ghost of Bernard, but he understood Bernard's
compulsion with Hannah. What man wouldn't
yearn after her? The sweet motion of her walk,
her proud carriage, the inordinate grace of her
movements, her perfect body, those high round
breasts, that curved waist that flowed so beautifully into her rounded hips.

He took her hand and held it in his to look at
it. It was half the size of his. His hands were
tough, brown, with a sprinkling of dark hair on
the backs and along the knuckles of his fingers,
while hers were ivory grace. He lifted her hand
to his mouth and turned the palm to touch it with
his tongue.

Her eyes widened at her body's response, and
he knew no other man had ever done that to her.
His body was as taut as it could be, and she
wasn't really conscious of how she affected him.
She was virginal. In spite of having had a child,
she was an innocent.

She made him feel very tender toward her. He
felt protective in a way no other woman had ever

commanded of his feelings. There hadn't been many who had touched his life, but Hannah was something else altogether. He smiled into her eyes. "Come down and let me out. We'll go around and check the locks downstairs."

He was leaving?

He saw her distress and was thrilled by it. "Would you like one more kiss?" He smiled as she swallowed and nodded.

Since he was leaving, he held nothing back from that kiss. He allowed his passion to rise, and he moved his hands on her in skilled caresses. He surprised himself with his skill. It wasn't that he was so knowledgeable, but that was how he wanted to touch her, this woman who bemused him so. This enchantress. His woman.

They went downstairs rather slowly. Her equilibrium wasn't reliable, and he was having trouble just moving. The lock check was his job, and he knew what he was doing; she simply trailed along, not paying any attention.

While they were in the kitchen, Lillian came home and spoke into the CB in the entrance hall. She smiled ethereally at the silent pair who came from the kitchen to watch her as she floated upstairs as if in a trance.

Max guessed, "They made up."

Quite seriously, Hannah nodded agreement.

"Good thing I didn't plan to stay tonight. I never dreamed Pete would allow Lillian to leave."

"She'd never spend the night."

"Not right away," he countered.

"Never."

"We can't actually move Amanda out after I move in. She needs us. And the family has set up that trust for Geo, so we couldn't just take that and kick Amanda out."

"I didn't intend to ask Miss Phillips to leave."

"If she gets her hearing back, we may have to be reasonably quiet as I chase you around the house."

"Why, Max, you couldn't do that."

"Oh, yes," he said comfortably. "There's just a time when a man has to chase a woman. So she runs and squeals."

But into Hannah's mind came the memory of Bernard tearing at her clothes, and she shivered.

Max was aware that her shiver wasn't desire clamoring for release, it was the shiver of dread. He became very gentle, and spoke of other things in a slow voice. She did reply, but he didn't have her full attention.

How could he have been so stupid as to tease

about chasing and catching, when she'd told him how Bernard had raped her? He was a classic fool. Now she would tighten up the way she had at first. He'd have his work cut out for him to get her to relax and enjoy him, as he wanted her to. He just hoped he hadn't blown everything.

Seven

The police were especially needed on the Fourth for directing crowds and traffic and for quelling behavior that was not acceptable. Therefore, the Police Society picnic was on July third. Even then, not all the members could attend. It was a busy weekend for law-enforcement people and for the volunteers who helped at that time.

There had been some discussion in recent years to postpone the Society's picnic or having it at another time; but the roots of the organization had been set long ago, in a citizen's peacekeeping force, when there hadn't been as many people around and the holidays weren't as hectic. Tradition, at that long-ago time, set the day as one to salute peace as well as freedom. The Fourth was an important day for such a celebration, for it underlined how hard it is to keep both.

It rained. Partly cloudy skies had been predicted. How could anyone accurately predict the fickle Indiana weather? It rained buckets and, even though it was July, the wind blew up as cold as fall. Hannah looked out her bedroom window and knew right then that Lillian would not go to any lake. She knew as well that no one would go to any picnic on such a day. They would all stay there at the house in a happy little group of four. Lillian, Geo, Max and her. She was as gloomy as the day.

She got out of bed and pulled on a yellow sweater and jeans and put a yellow Alice band around her very light hair. Then she added lipstick and blush and put gold loops in her ears. That ought to give Max something to think about; she'd told him she seldom wore earrings.

Geo removed his cigar and observed, "Rain."

"Yep. We may have our picnic here."

She dressed Geo in cords and a sweater, then went down the hall to waken Miss Phillips. She was already up, sitting at her window, looking out at the day. Hannah moved so the old lady knew she was there, and smiled at her. Amanda Phillips made no response. The weather must depress her, Hannah thought as she straightened the bed, and she felt sorry for the older woman.

Then Amanda Phillips spoke. "I love this kind of day. When we were kids, we'd go to the attic and play dress-up. The rain would sound on the roof just above our heads, and it was a magic time."

Hannah turned and stared. That was more words than Miss Phillips had said to her in almost two whole years! It was hard to think of the silent old woman as a child laughing and playing dress-up with other children. Hannah wondered where the other children were now. All old or dead. How sad.

"It smells so delicious," Miss Phillips continued. "Breathe in, and you can believe in an earth goddess, all the marvelous earthy mysteries. And clean air." She gave Hannah a droll, cynical look. "Probably all polluted with acid and other killing chemicals. But it's also full of memories of great times."

That tough old bird of a stubborn woman was a romantic! She'd never bothered to share such thoughts before. How selfish of her! Hannah smiled a little and was still as she listened, hoping the old woman would go on. But Miss Phillips stood slowly and allowed Hannah to help her dress.

Lillian came from the bath and hurried around with last-minute packing for her holiday. She would still go in that weather? As Hannah took Geo downstairs to fix breakfast, she considered that Lillian would be going to the lake. That surprised Hannah briefly, but then, as organized and prompt as Lillian was, a little rain wouldn't ever deter her.

Following Miss Phillips, Lillian hurried into the kitchen, ate a quick breakfast, gathered her things and cheerily left!

Hannah wrote on the pad "intrepid". That was a new word for her. She felt it described Lillian. Miss Phillips nodded and went on eating. Hannah wrote hesitantly, "Will you talk to your family?"

Miss Phillips took her time in replying. When Hannah had given up on a reply, Miss Phillips said, "I'll see." Then she gave Hannah a stern look. "Don't you tell them I can talk."

Hannah wondered if Miss Phillips would continue to punish her family by not speaking. She was mad at them, so she wouldn't speak to them. People could be so difficult. Generally they punished themselves more than those who made them angry.

As she considered that wisdom, Hannah found her eyes on Geo, who was concentrating on eating scrambled eggs and fingers of toast. He was such a precious child, yet he had foolish grandparents who didn't want to know him. That was a new thought for Hannah. She had been feeling isolated by them, and for the first time she understood that they had isolated themselves.

Three of Miss Phillips's grandnephews came for her, laughing and acting glad to see her and being very kind. She accepted that stoically, and Hannah could have kicked her. All three found time to say to Hannah, "Thank you for caring for her." They wrapped Amanda carefully against the weather and held umbrellas for her protection; then one of them picked her up. They took her out and put her into the grand automobile—no one would call that marvelous thing a car—and they drove away.

For the first time in a long, long time, Geo and Hannah were alone in their house. Alone. How strange to think of being alone as a pleasure. Always before she had thought of it as rejection. Her thinking was changing. Soberly, she understood that it was Max's doing, that man who claimed never to intrude into anyone's life.

Smiling at the thought of Max, she went out to the garage and brought in armloads of wood to stack in the back hall. Then she built a fire in the living-room fireplace. The facing of the fireplace was walnut. It had been painted at one time, and one of these days Hannah was going to strip off all that paint and see the beauty of the wood.

Max came at ten, bringing excitement, a burst of wet air, and a male presence that filled that big house. He grinned and gave her a quick kiss and ruffled Geo's hair. "Since I'm such a clever man, I have the entire weekend free!" He beamed at her, and she felt serious qualms. "I've traded weekends so many times, and this weekend I called in all the IOUs. I was heartless." He gave a dirty laugh, and Geo joined in with a will.

Max had all sorts of plastic-wrapped goodies which he carried to the kitchen, where they sorted it all out. He had a predictable selection: potato salad, wine, wieners and buns, potato chips, baked beans, chili, a *whole* watermelon, and sparklers. "I thought we could do them on the front porch. That'll be our fireworks.

"Geo is a little young for fireworks."

"I'm not."

"This morning Miss Phillips talked about

when she was a child and playing dress-up in an attic with other children. The memory was a nice one. Not sad. Just a nice memory."

"When she...if she can hear again, she will probably be a delight."

"You're being sneaky with her. Tempting her into agreeing to have the exam."

"I'm glad she's out of the house today. She thinks I'm a fox in the chicken coop."

"Are you?" She smiled a little.

"Oh, yes." He kissed her, lifted his head to look at her, then kissed her again.

Even through the pleasure of his kiss, she had that feeling of alarm. Although she didn't end the kiss, she stiffened slightly.

He was aware of it. He had all weekend. No rush. He was going to do this right; but he would have her. He smiled. "You look like a sunbeam in this gloomy day."

"Come in by the fire."

He, too, was dressed for the chilly weather. "Ahhh..." He made the sound so eloquent. "Perfect." He looked around. "A cold, rainy day, a beautiful blonde, and a fire to watch. I suppose it's too early for the wine?"

She laughed. "I rarely drink."

"This is an occasion." His lashes were down

over his eyes, his face pleasant, his resolve sure.
"We'll have a little with lunch."

That big house was made for hide-and-seek
they traded off partnering Geo as both hunter
and hunted. They played cat and mouse, with
Max a big, stealthy cat, chasing Hannah and a
laughing Geo as the skittering mice.

Hannah had made the big pillows they put on
the floor in front of the fire, there they sprawled,
laughing. There wasn't much furniture, but the
Phillips's rug was a jewel on that wooden floor,
and there were the rocking chairs.

When the time came to eat, they laid down
aluminum foil to catch any splatter on the
hearth, then they roasted their wieners on sticks
over the hot coals of the dying fire. The meal
was eaten leisurely as the adults sipped the wine,
sitting there on a blanket by the fire, but they
ate the watermelon on the porch where the drip-
pings could be hosed away.

A sticky Geo chortled as Max carried him
through the house, up the stairs and to the bath,
where Hannah filled the tub. It was a contented
tired little boy who was rolled into his snug bed,
and he was asleep almost before they were out
of the room.

"You're very good with children." She had
become nervous. Would it be now?

He replied quite normally, "I'm brilliant with children." He led the way down the stairs, and she trailed along as he added, "I have nieces and nephews and cousins with little kids." Entering the dining room, he stood surveying her progress as he said modestly, "I am phenomenal."

"And modest?"

"All phenomenal men are modest." He gave her an aloof and superior look.

"And phenomenal women are modest?"

"Perhaps some are, but phenomenal women are unusual, so they tend to be braggy."

"Why do you say phenomenal women are unusual? Women and men aren't that different."

"Pish and tosh," he demurred. "People expect men to be phenomenal, and they are. Therefore, a man accepts that he is and doesn't make a fuss about it, but no one expects a woman to be phenomenal, and when she is, she tends to strut and crow about it."

"Women do not strut and crow."

"Cackle and squawk?" He frowned in his search for the perfect descriptive words. "Better go change your clothes, we're going to paint."

"Paint?" That did surprise her. In all of her thoughts about that weekend, somehow painting hadn't ever entered her head as one of the activities in which they'd indulge. She said it again, "Paint?"

Rather absently he replied, "Um-hummm. My things are in the car." He was wearing jeans but shed his sweater and rolled up the sleeves of his blue workshirt. He went out to his car and brought in folds of canvas and packages of plastic drop cloths.

He was going to *paint*! She went upstairs and changed into clean scruffies, then went downstairs again, rather amazed.

He had a boom box with cassettes, so they didn't talk much in the next two hours as they finished up the dining room. He used a big four-inch brush for the corners and along the molding, but on the walls and ceiling he used rollers with long handles. The entire room was done in a quarter of the time it would have taken her. The ceiling was done within a half hour, and the walls proved no contest at all. It was just astonishing. Muscles. Muscles were the answer—that and reach. He worked hard, with dispatch and no wasted motion.

Geo came downstairs in his footed, light flannel pajamas to watch them from the door. "Hi, Geo." Max smiled at Hannah's child. "I have something for you."

"No gifts," warned Hannah. "I can't stand

kids who greet people with, 'Watcha got for me?''"

"This is basic, it doesn't involve you because it's between Geo and me." He went to his load of equipment and unwrapped a plastic stack of yellow lengths. He fitted them together, taped the backs, and set up a very neat car track that had a centrifugal circle of track at the bottom of it. Max propped the top against the back of a chair. He showed Geo a small car, then put the car on the top of the track, and it went down, around the circle, and out across the bare floor.

Geo chortled and ran for the car. The two adults went back to painting. With only a pause to put a casserole together and—having plenty— to make a melon salad, they spent the rest of the time painting the back hall. They didn't hear anything from Geo except the sound of the little car, his busily retrieving feet, and yet another run of the car. Hannah said, "You're phenomenal."

Max said, "Yes." Hannah laughed and swatted his bottom. He gave her a smug smile and said, "I like aggressive women."

They bathed separately and changed their clothes before supper. When Geo was in fresh pajamas and the dishes were done, they again sat on pillows by a renewed fire. Max held Geo on his lap as he read from three old and tattered books. Geo didn't make it through the last story, but Max finished the story because it was one of his favorites.

As Max finished reading, he closed the book and looked up into Hannah's tender eyes. She said softly, "You're phenomenal."

He replied quite logically, "And I'm not even trying...yet." He lifted the sleeping boy and said, "Sit still." He carried Geo up the stairs, but he took so long that she went up after him. She met him in the hall. Quite deliberately then he told her, "Now I have a treat for you."

She was conscious that she still had a feeling of hesitation. Her lips parted, but she didn't say anything because she wasn't sure she could say that he would understand. She only looked at him, her eyes filled with uncertainty.

"I've brought a movie for us to watch. Let's take the TV and VCR down by the fire." He carried it all downstairs, set it up, arranged the fire and the pillows. Gathering his precious books he'd shared with Geo, he put them in a stack with his things. He put the tape in the VCR and they lay down side by side in the nest of pillows and the film began.

To her charmed bemusement, they spent the next several hours watching a beautifully told tale of magic spells and thwarted love. More than once, Hannah glanced at the man next to her. He watched the screen with concentrated interest, and she wondered how she'd ever managed to get involved with this complex and crafty man.

For his purpose of seduction, what more perfect film could he have selected than a beautiful, triumphant love story? When it was through, he smiled at her and yawned, stretching his magnificent body with slow relish. Then he clasped his hands under his head and said, "About time for me to leave, isn't it?"

He would leave *now*? He hadn't even kissed her. In all that solitude, of empty house and alone with her, he not only hadn't touched her, he hadn't even really kissed her. So she sat up and looked at him. When he didn't do anything but look back at her in a waiting way, she leaned over him so that her breasts had to touch his hard chest as she reached to kiss his cheek and then his mouth. He didn't fight.

Without moving his hands from behind his head, he kissed her back. He moved his mouth, and his muscles tensed. His breathing changed, and his throat made fascinating sounds of pleasure that touched her in places in her body. She disturbed him.

Putting her hands on his chest, she smoothed the material over his strong flesh, then stretched her upper body along his. As she almost lay on him, she put her hands into his thick hair with great pleasure, before kissing him again. She'd read about kisses like that—they really happened, they weren't made up. She began to tremble.

He nudged her cheek, kissing it, and moved his head so that he nuzzled her ear in a thrilling onslaught. But he didn't move his hands. She made urging sounds, and he whispered, "What do you want?"

"Hold me."

He said, "Ahhhhhh," in a great sigh, and his arms came down and around her to hold her to him, and his kiss was mind-boggling. In gentle, slow movements he turned her until they were lying face-to-face on their sides, and he skillfully unbuttoned her shirt, then his own. He was very slow. He ignored their shirts as he kissed her throat and moved his hand down her side to her thigh and back up along her ribs, but no farther.

Very gradually, he began to take the dominant position. But he took forever in the doing, and her mind was so involved with all the amazing feelings streaking and melting and licking through her body that she didn't entirely notice

what he was about—or that she was helping. She
had no idea how she thrilled him. She tugged
and pulled at his shoulders, her body squirmed
for position, she squeaked and gasped, and her
eager mouth kissed him.

Cleverly he opened his shirt so that, as he finally leaned over her, he could move her shirt
aside and gently rub his hard, hairy chest against
her highly sensitized naked breasts. She clutched
at him, her body curled, and she gasped. Then
he deliberately moved his evening whiskers under her ear, along her throat and down her chest
in slow swirls as he licked and kissed her excited, prickling flesh.

With only the fire's light, he worked her out
of her clothes, proving himself adept at getting
women out of their clothing with as much skill
as he'd used with Geo. But with her, Max was
so slow! Her fingers eager, she helped him to
undress. He was charmed by her; she was so
earnest, so unknowing in how seductive her ea-
gerness was to him. And she finally touched him
there in the firelight.

Then she bent her head and kissed him. After
that, the spiral of passion abandoned the wide
swirls as it narrowed in intensity and heightened.
Their hands grew more demanding, his breath
was hotter, and his mouth scalded her.

She couldn't stand anymore, and she pleaded, "Please…" not even realizing what she begged.

"What do you want?" he asked again.

She stopped to look up at him in a moment of comprehension. She wanted him desperately, and she told him so. "You!"

He paused only to protect her; then he took her with great care. She was so ready for him, but she was braced for the remembered tearing pain. As he sank into the heat of her, they were both startled by the ease with which her body accepted his invasion. It was lovely. Beautiful. Then he moved, and sensation mounted. She gasped again. No longer content with being only a part of him, she began to meet his thrusts, and the spiral narrowed again to reach…and reach…and reach! Her sound was such a marvel that he heard and joined her in that ecstatic peak, to hold her tightly as they floated free and shimmered in the aftershocks from touching paradise.

They lay together, still coupled. She made occasional tiny, sighing sounds of contentment. He gently nuzzled the side of her throat. He said, "You're fantastic."

"You're phenomenal."

"I was trying like hell that time."

"You made it." She assured him.

"I suppose you'll get braggy now that you find you're phenomenal, too."

"Was I, really?"

"Remarkably so." He kissed her cheek and laboriously shifted his weight onto his elbows.

"I had no...idea."

"Quite frankly, Hannah, neither did I. You're a remarkable lover."

"How much research have you done?"

"Just listening to the braggy ones."

"Women brag about this sort of thing?"

"No, men."

"I thought phenomenal men didn't brag."

"We're not talking talent, we're talking brag."

"You could brag. You are marvelous."

"And so are you. How lucky we are to have had this together. Thank you, Hannah."

"Ah, Max. You are an amazing man."

"Just trying to please, ma'am."

She laughed as he then yawned hugely. "It's early yet," she teased him. "How can you be so tired?"

"Well, Hannah, I do recall that I said it was time for me to leave some long time ago. After all, I've spent the day feeding you, painting, entertaining you and Geo. I was exhausted and only longed for sleep. But you—look what you did to me. Here I am, naked as a jaybird, lying in a pile of pillows on the floor in front of a fire. The *classic* seduction scene, and what are you doing? Naked and luscious. That's what you are. You're still trying to entice me."

"No, no."

"I can tell. I can tell when you're luring me. You want me to taste you, don't you. Like that? You want me to put my hands there, and do that, don't you."

"I don't...*think* so, but..."

"You want me to rub my whiskers on your tummy this way, right?"

"Behave."

"Too late. You have to be careful what you start when you're around a susceptible man." He laughed and did all the things she wanted. This time she wasn't quite so new or quite so hesitant or scared. She knew how good it could be, that this was a very different man. She enjoyed him, unafraid, relishing.

He took a long time showing her how her body could be touched and kissed, and he encouraged her to explore his. Her curiosity allowed her to be quite bold, and he took such pleasure in her venturings. She asked, "Do you like that?" He drew air through his teeth before he said, "It's...nice."

She touched him there again. And again. Her eyelids were heavy and her lips full, and her breasts tingled as she shimmered in other places as well. She lightly ran her fingernails along his skin, and asked if he liked that. He licked his lips and asked, "Like what?" So she did it another time or two. She gnawed at him gently here and there, and he turned her over and laid her flat.

She laughed and put her arms up over her head, and he had to sit back on his heels and look at her. She blushed, she felt so bold. But his eyes consumed her, and she loved it that she had such an effect on him, to make him, replete, want her again. So leisurely, so slowly, so gently he wooed her. And she returned all his caresses. Her hands on him followed the paths of his on her. And they made sweet tender love.

After a long time, their fires banked, they banked those in the fireplace, and she yawned. "Will you come over tomorrow?"

He looked at her, a little surprised. "I'm staying the night."

"Oh, no. You can't. The neighbors would all…know."

"We've been down here all this time with just firelight. Don't you think they know already?"

"Max! What am I to do about you." The question was rhetorical.

"Let me sleep in your bed with you."

"I've never...slept with a man."

"This will be a new experience, an expanding one."

"I can not."

"Sure? I am willing."

"Not...yet."

He patted her. "I'll be back tomorrow, early." He gathered his discarded clothing, dressed, and kissed her yet again. Then he left.

It touched her that he had gone as she'd asked. It would be very easy to allow all her behavioral barriers to collapse. He made love to her so naturally. How practiced was he in sleeping with a woman?

That hadn't really occurred to her. Did he sleep with other women? He was six years older than she. A passionate man. Had he had...many women? He could. He was very skilled. Look how he had allowed her to do his seducing for him. How clever he was with women. How...wonderful.

Max kept his promise and returned early the next morning. It was a dream weekend. The weather held—it was rotten. There was no reason to leave the house, so they didn't. Except to buy paint. They were to paint the front bedroom on the north side. Since they had to buy the paint, Max chose purple.

"Purple?" Her voice was doubtful.

"For passion. I've always been fond of purple. My mother once baked me a purple birthday cake, long ago. The least you can do is let me paint a room purple. When I move in, it can be my room."

"Lillian would be right next door."

"I won't hear her snore. The two closets are a buffer between the two rooms. Or I could sleep in your room with you."

"Max, you must not move into this house." Even she heard the change in her wordage. It had gone from he *could* not, to he *must* not.

He smiled and bought the purple paint.

Eight

Painted, the upstairs front bedroom was very purple. Color reflects to intensify, and in that room it intensified quite well. Actually, it was dreadful. Max looked around while Hannah stood there stunned by the outcome. Max said, "I've never chosen the color for a room before." He smiled and was so *pleased*.

After that, what could she say? She could close the room off until he'd forgotten about it, or was long gone; then it could be painted a pale yellow. She squinted and said, "It's very...purple."

He responded with satisfaction, "Yeah. Rich!"

How does a woman tell a man he has awful taste? Especially when he obviously likes *her*. "Will you be staying here for supper?"

He loved her oblique invitation and came over to hug her. "Like me, do you?"

"Well, it's just that this weekend the Citizens Watch Patrol schedule is tough to fill, with so much going on in the city for the Fourth. I just thought if you'd be here to stay with Geo, I could volunteer for a patrol."

"Baby-sit?" His face was still. She was treating him like a friend she could count on, and he liked it that she was conscientious about her part in her neighborhood.

But she thought she'd offended him. "It's just as tough to get sitters as people who will patrol on such a holiday weekend, you see. I just thought..."

"We'll let Geo sleep on the floor of the back seat, and we'll take the tour together."

"Oh, Max, would you?"

"A busman's holiday."

She grinned. "Yeah, a policeman doing patrol tour with a Citizens Watch. I'll call Pete. He'll be delighted."

They drew the midnight-to-two slot. Max said

he was disgruntled about the hours, so she chuckled and comforted him. "You can get to bed early, and you won't lose any sleep. You've worked very hard, with all this painting, and I know your muscles must ache."

He bit his lower lip to stop the grin, but his eyes danced with humor. "Yes. I do ache. I believe I need a massage. Let's lock Geo in the basement."

"I don't believe you're terribly paternal."

"Of all the nice little kids I know, Geo ranks right up there among the best. He's a good kid."

"I rather like you, Maxwell T. Simmons."

"But do you like me enough, that's the crux of this whole operation."

"Uh...how much is enough?"

"Will you take off all your clothes and lie down on this canvas drop cloth and help me initiate this fabulous purple room?"

She unbuttoned her shirt. He'd been teasing but, as she took him at his word, his surprise and delight flared his passion. "Where's Geo?"

"Watching a children's tape."

He closed the door and braced it, so that a little boy would have enough trouble opening it that they would be warned. He skinned out of his clothes and helped her to lie down. She lay there obediently and looked up. She was very exciting to him, and he had to fill his eyes with her before he knelt beside her and put his hands on her.

She said, "I'm a little dizzy."

"Hot dang, I don't think I've ever made a woman dizzy before."

"You did it to me last night. Today I think it's the paint smell."

"I'll hurry."

"Well, not necessarily."

Getting the paint off the various places on their bodies took some doing. And they did it with gradually escalating hilarity, but that time they separated to shower. They didn't make love, but they were loving.

That weekend, the knowledge of her growing love for Max sobered her now and again. As Geo napped, and she studied, Max used an NFL tape to help him get through the bleak, football-less desert of summer. She would look up from her papers and feast her eyes on him, lying there like a sultan on the pile of pillows.

He was very natural in this idyll, not the least bit awkward. He didn't 'company' chat, or wait to be directed. He did his share of everything, and much more. All that painting finished! She flinched over the purple room, but for Max she could even endure that.

He turned his head slowly, and his eyes rested on hers. The game on the VCR went on as they looked at one another, exchanging a long steady regard. When he slowly smiled just a little, it was like a caress. Her heart turned over.

That day she fixed a classic roast beef with potatoes, onions and carrots for dinner, the aroma wafting through the house. He'd breathe it, then breathe of her essence, and say, "The two best smells in the world."

"Smells?"

"Fragrances?"

"Aromas are food," she instructed. "Fragrances are for perfume or flowers."

"You're fragrant." He sniffed along her cheek toward her throat, moving his cheek along hers.

She hugged him and breathed of his skin.

Huskily he told her, "You stir me like no woman ever has. You excite me constantly."

"I don't mean to. I only like to breathe of you. Most men wear too much after-shave or cologne. They make my sinuses hurt. You smell so clean and...male. I love it."

"We're from a family of hunters. Men who wear after-shave have a hard time tracking. It's like men who smoke, or who've had coffee.

Their bodies, tobacco and breath are signals on the wind."

"What do you hunt?"

"Deer, possums, coons."

"That's cruel."

"We're having beef for dinner."

"I see."

"And we hunt dog packs. People have the mistaken notion that dogs can survive in the country, and they dump them along the roads. The dogs gather in packs and raid the farm animals. They don't know how to kill, so they mutilate animals. And the packs are diseased and miserable. People are cruel. Unreasonable people are called animals, but no animal would ever be so awful as people can be."

"That's why you're a cop?"

"A part of it. I'm going into politics. I needed this experience with city structure, law enforcement, and problems in a city. I'll go to the law school next, and get combined degrees in law and business management. It's part of the preparation, our family is very civic-minded. Serving in some capacity is taken for granted among Simmonses. We've been around a long time, and we feel the responsibility of helping."

Any dream Hannah had of marriage to Max died right then. A man who expected to do pub-

lic service could not be hampered by a woman
with an illegitimate child.

She was very quiet for a while. So quiet that
Max asked, "Are you all right?"

"Oh, yes. Just thinking."

"Very serious thoughts?"

Knowing more each day of the kind of person
he was, she said honestly, "You're a good man,
Max."

"I'll get better as we go along." He grinned
at her.

She not only began to understand Max, she
began to understand women who devoted their
lives to men. As independent as she was determined to become, she was beginning to understand how women could throw everything to the
winds to follow a special man.

The realization was very sobering. She could
be persuaded to live clandestinely on the edges
of this man's life, just to share a part of him.
That was a tough admission. But the knowledge
of how the world treated a woman who broke
the rules strengthened Hannah's determination to
resist such temptation and live her own life
proudly.

Her determination made the rest of the weekend painfully poignant to Hannah. She gathered
touches and glances and affection to last her. He

was charmed by her, and his tenderness became exquisite. He shared her delight over Geo, and he basked in her attention without any idea she was telling him a long goodbye.

After supper, in the gloomy, drizzly evening, they lit the sparklers on the front porch. Max had a great time writing in the air, the flowing fire making designs that lingered. Geo laughed as he sat on the swing, but he wasn't interested in holding one. Max got a bar of soap, stuck five sparklers in it and lit them all at once. It looked gorgeous.

After they tucked Geo in that night, they went to her bedroom and set the alarm for eleven-thirty. They made slow, marvelous love. He was enthralled. She held him so sweetly, and her kisses were so intense, that he was lifted to another plateau of emotion. It was a strange land for him.

He slept in her bed, and she relished the feel of him being with her. It would be the only time this could happen. She hated the alarm, but roused him when it went off. They dressed silently, gathered Geo and two blankets to pad the car floor, then went out into the misty, chilly night to begin their patrol.

Anyone in the neighborhood association could see that Max was with Hannah. When they got back to her house after a routine, dull two hours of patrol, Hannah knew that there were eyes that watched to see if he stayed. He carried Geo into the house and up the stairs. He kissed Hannah good-night—and left. She got into her empty bed and lay there holding his pillow and weeping. Who ever said love made the world go round? They were wrong. Her world had stopped.

He came the next morning dressed for church, and he went with her. People smiled and nodded, pleased there was a man with Hannah. She thought, if they only knew, she would be better off if she'd never met him. Of all the people at the mall that day, why was she the one he'd chosen to help him? She asked God about that, and she asked for strength. But after church she asked Max, "Why did you choose me that day you were after Lewis Turner?"

"I didn't see anyone else."

A little annoyed, she protested, "There were a hundred people along there."

He smiled over at her briefly as he drove along, and replied, "I saw only you."

How could she be angry with him after that? He admitted he was attracted to her. If things

had been different, she might even have had
hope he could love her.

They had the rest of the roast that noon. Geo
was taking his nap, Max was painting the upstairs bath a pale sea green and Hannah was
studying when Lillian came home from her
weekend. She greeted the pair and wrinkled her
nose at the paint smell, but she did admire the
color in the bath. However, Hannah took Lillian
to see the empty purple bedroom, and Lillian
was satisfyingly speechless.

Lillian hadn't been home ten minutes when
Pete called. Lillian *giggled*, put on a new red
raincoat and went over to Pete's. Hannah looked
significantly at Max, who burst out laughing.

Miss Phillips came home just after supper.
She was tired, and Hannah helped her to bed
early, placing a hot water bottle at her feet. Miss
Phillips sighed and smiled at Hannah.

It was a surprise when Max came for supper
the next night, and almost immediately Miss
Phillips grated at him, "I'll get my ears looked
at."

Max beamed. There was nothing that touched
Hannah's heart as much as the look on Max's
face when he was pleased. It made a woman try
to find ways to warrant that expression. It made
his look a prize to be won. But with all those

people around, one way was barred for Hannah. Her good-night kiss for Max was restrained, for she must begin to separate from him. She went to bed quite melancholy and restless.

Nothing works immediately, certainly not catching or losing a man. Waiting is the way of the world, and it's supposed to build patience. Miss Phillips couldn't get an appointment for a week, and it had to fit in Max's schedule because Miss Phillips wouldn't go with anyone else. Hannah could sympathize with that attitude.

The sun came out and the whole world steamed, growing corn in the Midwest but wilting people and setting off tempers. After supper, Max, Geo and Hannah went to visit Mr. Fuller. "I heard you were out on Citizens Watch patrol, Max. Learn anything?"

"Actually, I'm impressed. We wish all the neighborhoods were as organized and working the way this one is. It's great."

"Pete was glad to have you. Did he offer you a permanent slot for each weekend?"

"Oh, yes, he's a great organizer. I wonder if your area would be as diligent without him. You'll find out when he walks again."

Fuller inquired, "*When* he walks?"

"I'd bet on it."

Hannah listened and wondered what it would

take to get Pete to walk. Tie Lillian on one side of the room and disable the motorized bed? Could Pete make love to Lillian? Had he tried to make a pass at her when she had stormed home in such a temper? Whatever had happened, the problem was solved. Lillian bloomed—her cheeks were flushed, and her eyes sparkled. She and Pete were together a great deal, supposedly to perfect the watch programming.

Was there a little hanky-panky going on? Hannah thought. How was she any different from any other nosy neighbor? Well, she wasn't critical, just curious, and not a little envious.

Her and Max's good-night kisses were becoming difficult for them both. He didn't want friendly restraint, and she puzzled him. "What's wrong?" he asked. "Tell me what's the matter."

"Nothing."

"Something is."

"It's just so humid, and I'm tired."

"You're driving me crazy."

"Me, too," she answered honestly, but she was so forlorn that he tried to comfort her.

She said, "No. Don't."

But he saw her tears. "There has to be a reason for you to act this way."

"It's all just—hopeless."

"No, it isn't. Don't freeze up on me, Hannah. I think I should move in. The purple room is ready."

"No. You wouldn't keep your distance."

"So?"

"They would *know*! And I simply could not stand that. To have Miss Phillips look at me with suspicion... I would just die."

"You're too hyper about what other people think."

"I have good reasons."

"Well...yes... But, honey, I'm going out of my mind."

She cried, and he held her. That didn't help either of them. He didn't realize there was no solution.

So gradually Hannah withdrew from him. Her hands stayed on his shoulders as he kissed her, and her mouth was still and prim. Then she made their kisses casual and quickly done. Her hands only pressed against his chest, as if warding him off. It tore her heart out.

Tuesday of the following week, Max took Miss Phillips to the ear specialist. They were gone for almost two hours. Hannah was home from class with a new armload of mending from the cleaners when they arrived.

After opening the back door, Hannah began to speak. Then she realized Miss Phillips was in a dreadful temper, with her hands over her ears. Hannah asked in alarm, "What happened to her? What have you *done* to her?" She reached out to protect Miss Phillips, who was fit to be tied.

Max hushed Hannah as he brought Miss Phillips into the kitchen and turned quickly to stop the door from slamming closed. He eased it shut, then took Miss Phillips over to the table and sat her in a chair, whispering, "Soon now." He barely spoke as he whispered to Hannah, "She can hear, and she's been thrown into a maelstrom of noise! Do you have any of Geo's non-stick bubble gum?"

"Yes," Hannah whispered, her eyes enormous with sympathy and concern. The old lady was like a wet cat with its tail under a chair rocker. As Hannah opened the cabinet, the noise caused Miss Phillips to wince. Leaving it open, Hannah gave the gum to Max.

He eased it out of the noisy wrapper and gave it to Miss Phillips to chew in the silence. Max cupped his hand to receive the chewed and softened gum. He took a portion and wadded it into a ball...which he put into one of Miss Phillips's ears! He repeated the process, and as he eased the ball into her other ear he softly assured her,

"This will screen out most of the noise until you get used to it again, Amanda." He gently patted her cheek. "If you behave, I'll teach you to blow bubbles."

The old lady's tired and desperate eyes looked up at Max; then she turned her head and kissed his palm! Poor Miss Phillips had had all she could take.

"What *was* it?" Hannah urged.

"Wax." Max helped Miss Phillips up and said to her, "I'll carry you. You've done enough for one day." He lifted her and carried her up the stairs to her room, with Hannah following. Max laid Miss Phillips on her bed, Hannah removed her shoes and pulled a light spread over her, and they tiptoed out.

Going down the stairs, Hannah asked incredulously, "Just *wax*? That was all that was wrong?"

"The doctor said a lot of older people have that problem. It builds up gradually, and since they're old, people accept that they can't hear. They should never accept anything without a checkup. All this time, all these years, Amanda only had to have the wax taken out." He shook his head.

"If it hadn't been for you, she never would have."

"It happened to one of my great-uncles. We were made aware of such things happening. And old people hate to be fooled with and poked at. I think they're afraid the doctors will find something bad. Something that can't be fixed. So they just put up with what they have."

"Under the circumstances, didn't they have some earplugs or something to temporarily screen the noise for her?"

"Yeah, but they were all too big. The openings in Amanda's ears are very small. The doctor suggested the bubble gum. Actually, the act of chewing gum, or eating apples, helps to work wax loose."

"Such a simple thing. You're really something, Max. I...I admire you." She had almost said she loved him.

"Well, us phenomenal men need stroking now and again." He grinned at her, but she didn't respond. He said carefully, "I realize we've only known each other for almost two months. This has...was like wildfire between us. I knew it would be, that first day out at the mall. I've never had a woman take my mind the way you do, honey. It's very unsettling."

But she turned away and didn't reply. He didn't know what to do. Geo wakened from his nap, Hannah fixed supper, Max paced, Lillian came home, and Miss Phillips came down the stairs. She could hear. She listened, almost awed, as she heard all the sounds she heard. "Hannah," Miss Phillips's own voice was softer. "Hannah, you have a sweet voice."

Max beamed at her.

Geo took the change in stride. He made his usual one-word comments and concentrated on eating. Lillian's voice was hushed, and her pleasure in Miss Phillips's solved problem was so genuine that Miss Phillips smiled. Then the older woman said, "I heard the clock ticking."

Such an insignificant thing.

Max said, "For my great-uncle, it was a rooster crowing. He hadn't realized how long it had been since he'd heard a rooster crow."

Miss Phillips watched as Hannah automatically took up the pencil to write that note. Hannah paused, then realized it wasn't needed. She grinned at the others, then deliberately took the pad and pencil and put them into a drawer... making Miss Phillips wince at the sound of it closing.

Hearing didn't miraculously change Miss Phillips's personality. She swore them to secrecy, and after a day or so she went off to a family gathering. Those left behind almost died of curiosity. What was the old lady up to?

Would they ever know? Had she spoken the last time? Did she intend to trap them into saying harsh things about her by letting them think she still couldn't hear? She had a wickedly unfair advantage.

When Amanda Phillips came back to the house, Hannah asked, "How'd it go?" Miss Phillips ignored her, as was her custom, but she appeared subdued and went up to bed early.

While saying good night in the back hall, Max speculated, "Someone said she or he loved that old lady, and her conscience is giving her fits."

"Now how could you ever know that?"

He grinned. "Kiss me nicely."

She said regretfully, "I have a sore throat."

As sure as he stood there with her, he knew she lied. But why? he wondered. "Hannah, we very badly need to talk. What..."

Into the back hall came the sound of Pete's excited voice, and Hannah ran to the front hall to grab the CB to listen.

Like a general, Pete was directing his forces. Four intruders had been spotted carrying baseball bats. Was it the same four as before? Carrying his CB, a neighbor had recklessly gone out to challenge them. Pete had heard him ask, "Who are you? Where do you live? Why are you out here?" The four sassed, "What's it to you?'' and threatened the man. Other neighbors had rushed out, and the intruders had left. Max simply vanished out Hannah's back door as she listened to the CB.

She didn't see or hear from Max until he came for supper that next evening. He had gotten the license number of the intruders' car. The police were hunting for it. It was only a matter of time before they were known, for the police knew who owned the car. It was Max who found them.

Watching Max as the days passed, Hannah was more and more convinced that his future lay in public service. The whole world needed all the men like Max that could be found; not one must be distracted from helping. Max knew this and accepted that it was his duty to serve his community. He might even be president some day, and he couldn't be shackled to an unwed mother. It would only make it more difficult for him. She had to let him go.

Then Max's work schedule changed. He no longer came to supper every night, and they all missed him. The table conversation did continue, but it wasn't as interesting without the refreshing gust of Max to stimulate them in his non-intrusive manner.

Hannah suffered with her lovelorn moods.

She longed for him like a Victorian spinster with an unrequited love. Her appetite fell off, her cheekbones became gorgeous, her appearance fascinating.

They never met at lunch because her schedule was so varied. He had to sleep sometime, so he began to come for breakfast, which isn't the best visiting meal. Everyone was on a schedule except Amanda Phillips, who smiled, very amused by his plight. He would clean up the kitchen after Hannah and Geo left, and he would play chess with Amanda.

He painted, stripped woodwork, and lost weight. He looked leaner and meaner. Men don't pine, but Max did. He worried he would lose her. She made no real effort to be with him. He thought she'd tired of him.

Then word came that the criminal Max had helped capture at the shopping center, Lewis Turner, had escaped from prison.

Nine

Lewis Turner escaped from prison when the inmates had rioted. They had trashed their cellblock and set it on fire. There were prisoners who were victim to other prisoners. While the convicts had been sorted and moved, somehow Lewis Turner had slipped away. In all the turmoil, he'd had a head start before he was missed. An inmate's anonymous tip to the warden said Turner had sworn that if he ever got out of that place he'd get the little blonde who'd helped the cops at Byford's mall.

Max first heard of the threat when his supervisor said, "You know the little blond lady who walked across the mall with you when we got Turner? Well, he's said he'll get her." Max's muscles tensed, and stayed that way. Hannah's name hadn't been in the paper—how could Turner find her? He had people in Byford. Would they help him take revenge on Hannah? A nightmare began for Max.

Hannah didn't take the threat as seriously as Max, which nearly drove him crazy. He said, "You have to pay attention. You should skip school until this is settled. We'll have him in a couple of days at most, and you can work at home."

She scoffed. "You are unreasonable. I can't live that way. Do you want me to barricade the house? How about sandbags at the top of the stairs and machine guns?"

"Don't be frivolous."

Stalemate.

The chief of police came by with several aides, and Max included himself in the group. It was allowed. They suggested a policewoman take up Hannah's routine, and the boarders would have to leave the house. They could go to a hotel, and they'd have protection. It probably wouldn't be necessary, but better safe than sorry, as the saying goes.

* * *

Meanwhile, five blocks away, alone with his police scanner, his computer, his CW base and radio, Peter Hernandez found out about Turner. He said aloud, "Hannah's in danger?" *Then he got up off the bed,* saying, "Lillian's there!" He stood in the middle of the room for whole minutes before he realized what had happened! When he understood that he was actually standing—and that it wasn't another hallucination—he shivered with shock of it and then he cried. All alone in his house, the miracle had taken place.

And he made such a cake of himself that he thanked God he was alone. Brutus came to him to whine inquiringly, and Pete leaned down and petted his dog.

Only stern self-discipline and good sense prevented Pete from walking out of the house and over to Hannah's to find Lillian—who wouldn't be there but at work. How would he tell Lillian he could walk? It was tempting to be quite dramatic, to wait for her to come over and then simply stand up. But could he shock her like that? She loved him, and he needed to ease her into the realization of this miracle. Could he sit down and stand back up again? Could he?

He dreaded to consider the possibility that his standing had been a fluke. What if he'd been granted just this one last time to stand up? He had to know. He went to a guest chair, and he sat down. He sat! Then he pushed down on the arms of the chair and, as easily as if he had always done it, he stood up.

He walked. How astonishing to do that again! How would he tell anyone? After Lillian, who would he tell next? He went over to the window...and looked outside. It was one of the biggest thrills of his life. Who ever thinks to appreciate the simple things we take for granted?

He called Lillian at work. "Honey, could you leave the office now and come over? Something quite...amazing has happened."

"What?" she demanded. "Are you all right?"

"I couldn't be better. Come to me."

"You've won the Super Lotto game?"

"Even better."

"What?" she asked impatiently. "Tell me!" And he said, "Come see."

"You've conquered the watch program!"

He laughed. "Come see."

"Is this really important?"

"It is very important, Lillian. I ask that you come to me."

He almost died of suspense. Of course, Lillian tidied her desk before she left her office, so it took her close to an hour to get to Pete's. She had her own key, she was there so much, and it saved her waiting on the porch for his slow bed to move to the door to open it.

She came in hurriedly and strode through the rooms, calling, "Pete?"

He was on the bed, as he normally would be. She walked to him and leaned over to kiss him as she asked, "What can be so important?"

"Something has happened."

"If you've dragged me away from work for something foolish, Peter Hernandez, I shall be quite cross."

"This is important. I need you here at this time. Sit down, honey. In that chair over there."

She asked quickly, "You *are* all right?"

"I promise you I am."

She gave him a quick, intense study; then she went to the chair and sat down. "Tell me about this."

"I heard this morning that Lewis Turner has escaped from prison, and the warden had a tip that Turner swore revenge on the little blonde who helped the cops catch him. That was Hannah."

"I remember! Well, I'm glad you called me! I'll go right on over. Thank you—" She moved to stand up.

"Wait. I thought of Hannah, but then I thought of *you* living in that house, Lillian. And I stood up."

"He isn't after me, you know. I'm... You what?" she asked cautiously.

"Lillian, I can walk again."

Her face was all he could have asked. The fleeting expressions of astonishment, doubt, hope and celebration told him all he wanted to know. She did love him. Again she started to rise, wordless exclamations tumbling over each other.

"No, sit still." His voice was soft. "This time let me come to you."

At Hannah's, Max groused, "It would seem to me one little woman could be kind enough to allow the police force to tell her what she should do. We know our business, you're just damned stubborn."

"I am reasonable." That was her tart response. "I am adult. I know what I'm capable of handling. I am careful. I've been with the CCW for almost two years, and this is a careful neighborhood. The people around here are trained to be alert to strangers. They will watch very closely during this period. Turner might come to this area. If he does, the police are aware of what's going on, you're here, there is no reason on earth for me to hide somewhere else on an inmate's suggestion that Lewis Turner might be after me. I can't live my life on maybes.''

"Hannah, we've known each other for about two months. You mean...a great deal to me. I would be concerned for any citizen who was even this tentatively threatened. We take any threat seriously. You should think of Geo. Pay attention.''

"Someone would be with me no matter where I was. I would rather be in this neighborhood, which I know is committed to safety, than to be with strangers. The people around here like me. There's an exchange of concern, and I'm not alone. All these people in this area know who I am and will help if I'm in trouble.''

He grudgingly admitted, "There is a logic in what you say, but since I'm having a terrible time not scooping you up and taking you to Ohio, I've decided I'm moving in.''

"Now, Max...''

"This is police protection.''

"There are undoubtedly policewomen who could do this instead.''

He felt she didn't want him around. She'd made no response to his telling her she meant a great deal to him. She wanted someone else with her during this time, not him. He *had* to see her through this safely. He would get out when Turner was back in prison. Not before then. "I'm going to be here with you."

"It's nice you're a non-intrusive man. I'd hate to see what you'd be like as a man who interfered in other people's lives."

Because of their connections through the city, the Phillipses heard the rumor about Turner being after Hannah Calhoun. Their people consulted with the police, had the information on the layout of the house and grounds, and the usually stoic cop mentioned the purple room with an uncharacteristic blink. The grandnephews came to Hannah's house to fetch Miss Phillips out of danger. She refused to leave.

Looking apologetically at Max, who was in uniform, the grandnephews told Hannah, "We've hired some guards. On each shift, one will be in the—purple—room upstairs to watch the front of the house. Two will be in the top of the garage, to watch the back and the alley." They grinned at Hannah in real humor. "The guards should substitute for Aunt Amanda. She's a tiger when she's roused." One leaned over and kissed the old lady's cheek.

That was a pretty rash comment to make in front of Miss Phillips, and the couple was surprised the nephews had spoken in such a free manner. One nephew had taken a gold pen from his pocket and a pad on which he printed a paragraph, which he held for Miss Phillips to read. *Then* Max and Hannah realized the old lady had kept it secret that she could hear.

Hannah gave Miss Phillips a disgruntled but amusedly chiding look, and the old lady narrowed her eyes in stern command. They were not to spill the beans. Then Miss Phillips handed the pad back to her nephew and shook her head. She hadn't *spoken* to her family, either! What a difficult old woman.

The nephews wrote about the guards and obligations Miss Phillips had to her family, and each time the old lady stubbornly refused to leave Hannah's house. So they told her the reports that Lewis Turner had been seen in Byford.

Turner was in Byford? Hannah raised her head, her nostrils flaring, and cast a stern look at Max. He hadn't told her that. But he was fascinated by Miss Phillips, who still pretended to her nephews she could neither hear nor speak; and being an unintrusive man, he was trying to figure a way to make her betray herself. Wicked, wicked man. He smiled. "Offer her a place back on the Philcane, Inc. board as a bribe,'' he put in lazily. Then he said quickly, "Watch her!"

She'd gasped and jerked her head around at Max, and she'd said, "Max..." before she could stop herself. She was furious!

"She can speak! She can hear!" The jubilation among her nephews was so honest that Miss Phillips flushed with pleasure that she couldn't disguise. The nephews hugged her, then Hannah. As Max glared and pulled Hannah from them, one nephew went to the phone to spread the news, but at Hannah's house pandemonium reigned.

"Say my name," one nephew teased. "Come on, Aunt Amanda. Tell me."

"You wicked boy!" she scolded, including them all but mostly glaring at Max. "You're incorrigible. And I went to school with your aunt Ceilly Simmons!" She meant he had no secrets from her because she knew silly Ceilly.

He smiled and retorted, unimpressed, "My Aunt Ceilly adores me."

Amanda Phillips snorted. "That's hardly a recommendation."

Max laughed, and Hannah's eyes clung to him. It was Max, yet again, in his practiced repulsion of the temptation to intrude. Oh yes, it was his doing. Ah, Max.

With Amanda hearing and speaking, the nephews felt no need to do more than give good reasons for her to leave. Especially with the guards there in her place. They simply took her away, laughing affectionately over her protests.

Max locked the door after them and turned to Hannah. "I wish I had the courage to do exactly that to you."

"I'd sue."

"How did you ever have such a cooperative child?"

She didn't reply.

He said firmly, "The Phillips man will be upstairs; you'll be safe enough from me." She made no comment, no protest. He gave her ample time before he added, "I'll sleep down here."

That was the second day that Turner was loose. The CB almost crackled with the excitement. Hannah thought the response of the neighborhood association was fantastic and just a little excessive. The patrols had been routine for some time, so the new threat gave added interest. Everyone was excitedly taking licence numbers of unfamiliar cars until Max mentioned to Pete that strange cars going by Hannah's house were undercover patrols.

Pete replied that Lillian would stay with him until the crisis was past. They just about had the watch program complete, and were already using it. It was phenomenal.

"And modest?" Hannah smiled at Max. "All phenomenal things are modest."

"Only phenomenal men."

"Max..." she began tenderly, but then she stopped and turned away.

"What, Hannah," he urged. "Tell me what you started to say."

She shook her head and went to check out the refrigerator.

He followed to tell her, "The city pays my food—out like this. I asked..." Suddenly he grabbed her shoulder and dragged her to the floor, taking out his gun!

She gasped, sprawled on the floor. "What is it?"

He looked out the window like a cop on TV, then ducked down without replying.

A man came to the back door and knocked. Max warned, "Careful."

"Right. We're the Phillips people. We're taking up positions. The upstairs man needs to be inside. May he come in?"

"Put ID in the mail slot in the front door. I'll let you know."

Max's police radio said, "Phillips men in place." But Max didn't reply. He pushed Hannah into the back hall and disappeared. She went up the back stairs to Geo, who was still napping.

Was she doing the right thing to insist on staying? This was her home. Her own place. She could not bring herself to leave it. She looked at her son; he too would stay.

From downstairs, Max shouted, *"Hannah!"*

She went to the top of the stairs and called down, "Here."

Max and another man, a Phillips guard, came up the stairs. The guard nodded to Hannah and went to the front bedroom. He hesitated for a minute as he opened the door to the purple room, and went inside, but he left the door open.

Max had the strong fingers of his left hand clamped around Hannah's upper right arm. Through his teeth he snarled, "When I put you someplace, you stay there."

This was a different Max. He awed her a little, but her temper came to her rescue and she snarled back, "Then put me with Geo."

In her short life, Hannah already knew that there were all kinds of waiting. Anticipation. The dreaded things are troublesome, especially if there is no set time limit to the endurance. You wanted it over with as soon as possible.

Max, Hannah, Geo and the Phillips men stayed at the house. The only calm ones in her house were the Phillips men. Although the Phillips men were efficient, businesslike and punctual, Hannah wondered if those walls in the purple bedroom—reflecting more and more color to each other, intensifying endlessly—could be causing brain damage to the guards who took turns spending time in that room.

She was positive of it, but she couldn't consult with Max, because then he would know she wasn't pleased with the color he'd chosen, and that might hurt his feelings. He'd never before been allowed to choose the color of a room— she now understood why.

The CB was left on. They could hear the reports to the base, which was Pete. Hannah recognized all the familiar voices; they were a little tense, conscious that they were doing something important. They were handling it well. And Lillian called Hannah. "Do you need me?"

"Thank you, but no. Max is here."

"Hannah, Pete can walk."

Hannah whooped and laughed with gladness, and the CB was busy as listeners exclaimed and the word spread. It was a marvel that everyone celebrated. Without thinking, Hannah flung her arms around Max, and his own closed around her in such anguish, such tenseness that he squeezed the breath from her.

She could have kicked herself. She'd been so careful to keep away from him, but he was still obviously attracted. She needed to keep distance between them, but her body took such pleasure in being against his. How marvelous it was to be held by him. She eased away, blushing, and awkwardly turned from him, subdued.

So, thought Max, she hadn't meant to hug *him*. It was just the excitement of Pete's regaining his ability to walk. That first night, when he'd been with her, they'd gone to Pete's to retrieve Geo. Did Hannah love Pete? Had she backed off when Lillian and Pete had begun to be interested in each other? As he watched and waited, he anguished over Hannah.

Since the Phillips men brought their own food with them, Hannah cooked only for Max, Geo and herself. One of the pluses of having Max trapped there was that he didn't surprise her with any of his horrendous food choices. She understood that he was impulsively generous, but he hadn't learned to be practical.

As he talked to Geo, or played with the cars

on the yellow ramp he'd made for her son, or sat reading to the boy, Hannah watched him with forlorn, hungry eyes. Why couldn't she have met him four years ago?

Every time he felt her watching him he glanced up, but she would then turn away. Finally he didn't look up. What did she see as she studied him? If she looked at him so steadily, so earnestly, wouldn't that indicate that she cared about him? Then why had she withdrawn from him?

To him, that weekend of the Fourth had seemed like heaven. Hadn't it been good for her? He'd been sure she'd accepted him as her lover, that he'd pleased her. Why had she drawn away from him? She was so perfect. How could he start again? Knowing she was watching him, he turned deliberately and looked back. How could a man tell a woman he loved her when she acted as if she didn't care at all?

She fed him chicken. Fried, or in rice, or with noodles. He brought in the largess from her garden, and they had fresh tomatoes, green peppers and wax beans. She lovingly baked him pies with her heart full of caring. The pies were of rhubarb, of strawberry, of raw shredded apple in a baked crust with cinnamon, a touch of nutmeg and lemon sugar, served with whipped cream.

On hot steamy days she fed him cold cucumber soup with sausage patties, summer yams and wax beans. She fed him steak, a large baked potato with sour cream, and a garden salad.

And the days went by.

"This is silly," she protested to Max. "Turner is long gone. He's probably in South America by now. I simply must take up my life again. I'm wasting all these people's time."

"We're staying."

"This has to be costing the Phillipses a mint!"

"You're worth it."

"Oh, Max." Her eyes were so tender.

Maybe, he thought, if he could stay there long enough, just propinquity might draw her to him. She could become so used to him that he could get close to her again.

The whole time was torture for Hannah. She'd given him up. Now there he was, all the time—his eyelashes screening his eyes as he read to Geo. His big hands moving so easily. She wanted them moving on her, touching her again, sliding over her bare skin to rub over her breasts and hold her head for his kisses. His mouth was so tempting to her. He was perfectly gorgeous, his body so beautifully male, so near, so... Thank goodness the Phillips man was upstairs.

If he wasn't, there was no telling what she might do. Attack Max, that's what. How startled he'd be.

She knew she could have him again, but it would be such a foolish thing to do. Nothing could ever come of it but an affair. It was better this way. She was giving him up for his own good. He needed to be free to go on with his plans of public service before he could be ensnared by her and Geo.

He could learn to love them. He was a good and honorable man. How unfortunate that, through a fluke, she was not suitable for him. Any opponent could use her past in sly ways that could thwart Max's goals. Ah, how she loved him.

So they were going through a terrible time, trapped together, at odds, suffering.

Geo, however, was having a marvelous time. His mother was home all day and all night, and Max was there. Geo laughed and chugged around and gave up "cigars." Max didn't smoke, and Max was his hero. He would climb up on Max's lap as if it were the most natural thing in the world. He treated the man as if he were his.

Max hugged Geo and rolled him around on the floor, carried him on his shoulders and showed him things. There was a ladybug on the windowsill, and a cat stalking through the yard. He taught Geo words, good words, strings of words, and he read to Geo.

There was no indication that Tuesday was any different. The time had passed, and Hannah had settled into the watch. Max, however, was strung up like a tensioned wire. The first call to Pete was routine. A watcher said, "A man walking up the alley on the east perimeter."

Pete called three neighbors before one saw him. One wasn't home, another's view was blocked, and the third was in the tub so the figure was already farther along.

"I think it's a road repairman. He's wearing a helmet."

Then there was another report. "Pete, there's a man slinking in from the south. Two alleys over from Hannah. White, tall, lanky. No, he's looking in trash cans. There's a car following. They're probably trash gleaners."

Pete had the grid on his screen, with two Vs indicating the strangers.

"A car coming into south section. Not one of the regulars. Blue Impala, right fender crumpled. Four door. Two men."

"One of ours," a gritty voice interrupted.

Then a woman's voice, "Three-eighteen, calling CW base?"

"CW base, go ahead, three-eighteen."

"Pete, I'm not certain, and this is probably silly, but it nags at me, and I probably ought to tell you. I'm just not sure, but I think someone might have got out of that brown car, the one following the trash picker. That back door wasn't latched when it passed me."

That electrified Max.

The CB went on intermittently as Max ran to the stairs and called to the Phillips man, "Did you hear?"

"Right."

Max turned to Hannah. "Take Geo and sit in the middle of the back stairs. *Now!*"

So Max went into the south study, just as Turner broke the glass door panel to the side porch and reached inside. And Max *snarled!*

Turner looked up, startled, then turned to flee toward the alley. Max burst from the door and leaped past the steps, yelling at the garage-based Phillips men, "He's mine!"

The chase was like one between a coyote and a rabbit. Turner dodged and ran and turned back, with Max on his tail. Max caught him in the alley. Both were running so fast that when Max leaped on Turner's back, Turner fell flat out, and

Max rode him like a sled on the uneven, roughly broken alley surface.

It took a while to get everything tidy, to do all the paperwork and cancel all the alerts. Max went down to the station with the prisoner. In Hannah's neighborhood the people gathered, talking, laughing, exclaiming over all the excitement, over Pete, and saying, "Now what do we do for entertainment?" They all drifted over to Pete's to see him walk.

Amanda called to say the Phillips men would stay in the garage another day or so, just to be sure. She was going up to the Phillips's summer place in Michigan, and would be back in a week or two. She'd call.

Lillian came by and hugged Hannah wordlessly, then squatted down and held Geo's hand. She told Hannah, "If you don't need me here, I'm moving in with Pete. We're going to get married. Will you stand up with me?"

With happy tears Hannah said, "I'd be proud."

Others came by to show they'd been a part of her protection, and Hannah was very touched by all their concern. She was glad she hadn't left the neighborhood. It is the sharing of common things and teamwork that build a community, and to share danger is another way. Now her neighbors felt free to show their affection for Hannah. They had helped her, and it made them closer to her and to each other. It wouldn't all be agreement, sweetness and light; there would still be quarrels, but all "families" had disagreements.

Alone with Geo, Hannah thought of those things and of Max. How dangerous he had been! Men are different. She had watched the capture, for she'd found she could not stay on the stairs. She'd admonished Geo to sit still, and he had. The games of hide-and-seek had paid off. But she'd run to the morning room, then to the back rooms, keeping Max in sight.

That cat-and-mouse chase! It had been so strange to watch two deadly men in that pleasant backyard in the late afternoon of a summer day. Cop and convict in a *serious* chase. The muscle power, the deadliness of it. And Max won. Of course. That was just how she felt—when it was over. She smiled and thought, naturally, he'd won. But she was exhausted from how riveted she'd been on Max winning.

She fed Geo, but she wasn't hungry. The CB murmured occasionally. People were still a little keyed up. She felt so oddly alone in the darkening of that summer evening. Almost...let down, and a little weepy. There was no longer any reason for Max to come back.

She allowed Geo to play for a long time in his bath, and he loved it. He had such a nice chortle. She sat and watched her son. She was glad she had him, and as much as she suffered now, she was glad she'd known Max.

It was almost ten when Hannah heard the back door open. She raised up from her place of gloom in the unlighted living room, tense and afraid. She heard the step, then Max's voice: "Hannah?"

She went to him in a rush. He opened his arms, and she didn't even hesitate. She went to him, into his arms, to cling to him as his arms closed around her and his head bent to hers. Her breath was uneven with emotion. Tears crept into her eyes. He was there.

Ten

Max and Hannah stood for a long time just holding each other. It was as if their cells absorbed the need to be together, like water in a desert. They were together. There was no misunderstanding then; they knew each loved the other. Their problem was still a barrier, but the love was there. Full-blown, marvelous…needful.

This time their love was different. It wasn't from desire and attraction; it was fulfillment of true love. Without the need to discuss it or question, they went up to Hannah's room. There they slowly removed each other's clothing. Max was still in uniform, so his clothing was much more complicated and he had to help her. His holster went over the bedpost, and the gun was a reminder that nothing had changed. He was a man committed to community causes.

But he was there with her.

Hannah's eyes stayed glued to Max in the dim light of her room. He was unsheathed from the concealing clothing, and stood before her so beautifully male. The thrill of him rippled along her nerve ends as her eyes feasted on her love. His lash-shadowed eyes, his unruly hair, his jaw, that lower lip. The V shape of him, and the muscles that rolled so sweetly beneath his flesh. His strong arms and legs, his hairy chest and stomach, his blatant masculinity. She reached out a hand to him.

He took her small hand into his large one, his own eyes covering her precious body, her halo of sunlight hair, her slender throat so fragile. His eyes moved down her body to the indentation of her navel and the lure of the fluff of pale curls at the apex of her long smooth legs. How graceful she was, how lovely, how female.

With his big feet planted, he tugged on her hand to draw her to him, and she took those steps with little urging. He put his hands at the bottom of her ribs, his fingers pressing her

nearer. She laid her hands on his chest, slowly
moving her fingers in the pleasure of touching
him. All of her yearned for him.

It was as if they followed a formal pattern of
love. They were slow in their exquisite movements. They kissed, and parted to look at each
other, then kissed again. His hands moved up
under her breasts and over the sides as his palms
slid up under her arms to nudge them up so that
her hands went to his head.

He drew her closer so that their bodies melded
together, her cool flesh scalding his hot skin.
How could that be? It was so. He held her tightly
then, one big hand spread on her back between
her shoulders, the other at the curve of her spine,
pressing her to him.

As they slowly moved, they panted. They
trembled and shivered. Their skins were sensitive to each nuance of touch. Their minds were
awash in sensuality, the feel, the sensation, the
thrill of need, the delicious ache of wanting.

He smoothed her hair back to kiss her face.
He touched her cheek with his fingertips. He put
his palms to the back of her head and his kisses
became exceedingly erotic.

To feel the play of his muscles under her
hands, she moved her palms slowly and with
relish. He was so male. She moved against his

body, wanting to feel the texture of his hair-shadowed flesh, loving the feel of his need, as her honey flowed. Her breasts tautened in her desire for him, and the nipples were like satin puffs to attract his touch.

He laid her down on the bed and moved close to her. With care each explored the other with palms and fingers and touchings. Their mouths caressed, their breaths gasped, and their throats sounded deep, pleasured murmurs.

When at last he rose above her, she opened to him and accepted him eagerly, her hands on his hard bottom pressing him deeply into her. They had to pause as they caught their breath and steadied themselves. Then they kissed with gentle kisses, which accelerated, their mouths opening more greedily, their movements quickening until they rode wildly in a mounting exhilaration in their thrilling ride to ecstasy. Tensed muscles rigid, they clung as they fell back through the vortex in a series of thundering afterthrills that rippled through their sated bodies but which finally dropped them back on the rumpled bed, limp, replete, still clasped together.

His breath unsteady, his voice trembling, Max said huskily, "My love."

And before she could stop herself, Hannah said in turn, "Oh, Max, I love you so."

He kissed her sweetly, sweetly, then again. His breathing still harsh, his heart thundering, he propped himself up on his elbows to hold her head between his hands. "You love me?"

In despair, she looked up at him with tragic eyes.

He smiled, and in a gentle voice he urged, "Say it again."

She put her arms up around his shoulders and pulled him down to her as she said tearfully, "Oh, Max." But she'd hidden her face in this throat.

He tried to peel her away enough to see her face, but she clung there, hidden. His deep chuckle was one of triumph, and he coaxed, "Tell me again. I have to hear you say it. I can't believe you love me. Tell me."

She said, "Oh Max…"

"Hey, what's so terrible about loving me? I'm not too bad. I like kids, I have all the natural instincts, I'm a good citizen, I never interfere…"

Even then that made her laugh, but she was choking on tears. He had no idea why their love should make her cry. He assumed it was from all she'd been through with the threat of Turner. Was she…had she worried about his own involvement? Most cops' wives worried. "You weren't worried about me, were you?"

The man asked that. He was the one who went to the hospital for stitches and then retrieved the bloody handkerchief to scare her. She put her head back and looked up at him finally. He was such a marvelous man. She loved him without any reservation, and would be his mistress for as long as he wanted. She would never allow him to know the qualms she felt about their relationship, and she would give her love to him free and clear.

"You worried about me?" he coaxed.

"I worried about that rabbit you chased all over my backyard."

He pressed into her with thickening interest. "And me? You worried about me?" Then he tensed, and his voice changed, "How did you know I chased him all over your yard? Hannah Calhoun, did you come out of that stairwell?"

"You might have needed me."

"Damn it, woman! I told you to stay put!"

"I am pretty 'put' right now."

"I told you not to move!"

"You don't want me to do...this?"

"Now, Hannah..."

"Or...how about...this? Couldn't I move... that way?"

He groaned.

She wriggled, then braced, and since he was lax and willing, she turned him over onto his back so that she was on top. Then she set about seeing how she wasn't supposed to move or do anything. She had to do that, if only to understand the limitations he was supposedly placing on her. She just needed to know how much she was allowed, but she couldn't find anything he complained about or stopped or...objected to. He even cooperated.

It was after midnight when they bathed each other with loving care. With sweet delight they told each other of their love. It was a relief to say it aloud and to the other. They smiled as they each agreed how fast it had happened. When? He said it was with his first sight of her, out at the shopping center. He'd seen no other person there.

When they went back into Hannah's room, she opened the closet door and showed him his picture taped there. Nothing could have convinced him more completely as the fact that she'd saved the newspaper picture of them together. "It was fate, that day."

In the humid night, they changed the wrinkled, dampened sheets on Hannah's bed before climbing back into it, into each other's arms, to sleep. To waken to find each other, so thrillingly near, to love and sleep again.

They wakened again at dawn and smiled. She told him, "You are a greedy man."

"I am not. It's just I had a lot of loving backed up, Hard-hearted Hannah. You hadn't been taking good care of me for a long time." Then he asked, "Why did you draw away from me, honey? Why did you doubt me?"

"How could you love me?"

"How could I not?"

So they didn't actually get to the core of their estrangement. It was enough that it was past.

All three went to witness Pete standing up and walking. He cheerfully complained that he was getting all the exercise he needed just showing off. They talked about his returning to the job that had caused him to be hurt. Could he?

"It'll have to be faced. I think I can."

Then, of course, "What about the CW base? The Citizens Watch? Would you still run that?"

"We'll split it up. Fran will take eight hours. Beth eight, and I'll take the night swing. I need one more person."

"I can't do it right away," Hannah told Pete. "But I plan to work at home, and I should be able to be relief. Like during lunch or dinner. That kind of thing."

"Good." Pete smiled at Hannah; then, as always, his eyes went to Lillian. "It'll all work out."

For Geo, there wasn't anything different about having Max around. He was simply pleased that Max was with them, and accepted his presence without clinging or clamoring for attention. After having given him up, Hannah had trouble believing Max was there. Her eyes went to him constantly, much as Pete's went to Lillian. Obviously Pete was as amazed that Lillian was with him as Hannah was that Max was in her house.

The Phillips men left the garage after another three days. Lillian was with Pete, Amanda in Michigan. Max went back on duty the next day. He was quite naturally at the house when he was off-duty, and he slept with Hannah. It was an idyll.

Hannah was back in school, finishing up the last of her classes. With Lillian gone and Amanda cordially reunited with her family, Hannah assumed she'd lost both her boarders. She needed to set up her business as soon as possible. Her adviser at school helped her to plot her approach, and suggested which size businesses she should solicit. She suggested the exact method of showing potential clients what Hannah could offer small businesses so that they would be relieved of the nitty-gritty of records and billing. Hannah began.

It was quite exhilarating. She was personable confident, and had been well taught. She knew what she was doing and what small businesses needed.

Max said, "You don't have to work. I'll take care of you. I make decent money, and I have a small private income." He smiled at that. It was private amusement over the 'small,' but it appeared that he was simply cheerful and willing to care for her. He said, "We'll be married as soon as we can arrange it."

"Married?"

He was also amazed. "Why does that surprise you? Do you think I'm going to let this house slip through my fingers? A wife who is fertile and willing? Who cooks and cleans and sews and gardens? I'm not a fool, you know."

"Oh, Max…"

Very gently he asked her, "Don't you want to marry me?"

"Oh, Max…"

How could she give him up? How could she let him go? How could she ruin his life? Didn't he realize how she could wreck all his plans? She anguished over him and over his dear proposal. He wanted to marry her! She said to him, "We'll think about it."

"We can practice. That's important, too. I need practice so you'll know I'm no shirker in the finer, more tedious aspects of married life."

That was all true. He devoted himself to the finer, more delicious aspects of practice, but he also talked to her, told her about his job and about the things he saw. They talked about kids who needed help, women who were abused, old people who lived in neighborhoods that scared them. He talked about solutions, about how things could be changed. And she listened with ice touching her spine. She was only deluding herself by considering marriage, by allowing herself to dream for a while—just a little longer.

It was wonderful to share a house with Max, to waken in his arms, to eat breakfast together. She wouldn't see him again until late in the night, for his shift began in the afternoon, but she knew he would come to her.

He moved some of his clothes in. She suggested, "Why don't you keep your things in the closet in the purple room?"

He carried his case there and looked around the empty room as she sorted hangers for him. He said, "Maybe the room's just a bit dark. Perhaps we should have chosen a lighter shade?"

Thoughtfully she looked around the ghastly room and asked, "What do you think?"

"Furniture and yellow drapes would tone it down. Naw. It's perfect. Rich."

She had a fleeting series of mind-stunning images of Max-decorated rooms, in an entire house. Her skin was suddenly covered with goosebumps. To make up for thinking so badly of his taste, she told him staunchly, "I do love you."

"We could move into this room."

Almost too quickly she replied, "No!" Then her tongue stumbled on, "I love the southern windows, in my room, and the sun in the winter." Brilliant!

"We should put up shades. The morning sun could fade the walls in here!"

She looked around in fresh hope, but she knew better. The paint was fadeproof. It would take five coats of pale yellow to cover it. By then, termites could eat away the wood, but the paint would still be thick enough; it would stand solid, and they'd never know the wood was gone.

Then Max said, "My mother and aunt are coming to see you next week." He grinned at her with pleasure. "They're anxious to meet you."

She was stunned.

Max came to her and kissed her. "I'm glad I know you. You're so precious."

But all Hannah could think of was that they would need to know about her. She couldn't hide Geo or lie. They would have to know, and they'd never allow Max to marry her. She became distracted, and something inside her shriveled up, dying.

When Amanda Phillips returned, Hannah greeted her in some surprise, "Well, hello!" Hannah had fully expected that Miss Phillips would send for her things and move out. Perhaps she'd come to do just that.

Miss Phillips looked at Hannah and almost smiled. "The lake was nice. A good breeze." She looked around thoughtfully. "Nice to be home."

That startled Hannah. Miss Phillips considered her room as her home?

Miss Phillips inquired, "Any other trouble?"

"You were very kind to provide the guards."

"They never had enough to do. It was good for them. A little variety. They're up at the lake this week with their families." She gave a garish grin, showing her good strong teeth. "One of the perks."

"Some tea?"

Miss Phillips pierced her with a sharp glance. "Isn't dinner ready?"

"Soon."

"I...like your cooking."

What a grudging admission. Hannah smiled, her amusement almost out of hand, and replied, "I've missed you."

"Huh!" It was a short sound, almost a bark. Miss Phillips trailed Hannah into the kitchen, tapped Geo on the head with her pointer finger, and sat at the table. "Where's Lillian? She can't be tardy?"

So Hannah had to tell Miss Phillips all the news. That Pete could walk again, and his apprehensions about going back to work as a fireman. Could he do it, or would he be afraid?

"He'll be all right. What about Lillian?"

Hannah turned at the sink and smiled at the old lady. "She's going to marry Pete, and she's asked me to be her attendant."

Miss Phillips nodded.

Hannah served her strawberries, with a sprig of mint to decorate the plate. Then she washed Geo's hands and waited as he crawled up on his chair. He looked his strawberries over, then began to eat.

There was a silence, then Miss Phillips inquired in studied casualness, "Max still around?"

"He...has asked me to marry him."

"Another bride!"

And it all came spilling out. About how the Simmonses were public-minded, how they ran for office. That she was an unwed mother—think what the opponents would do with that! She would ruin his chances. His family would never accept her. They were close, and Max loved them, but if he married her he would do as the Bible said and cleave only unto her. His family would then be torn apart. His mother and aunt were coming in two days, and what was she ever going to do? How was she to tell them? She cried and Geo joined in and Miss Phillips commanded them both to be quiet!

Geo obeyed right away, since he had no idea why he was crying, but Hannah was anguished and tormented and she had a tougher time of it. Silence reigned except for an occasional, heart-tearing, shivering breath from Hannah. It would have melted any icy heart...if Amanda Phillips had possessed one.

It was especially difficult for Hannah, for she still had one more thing to tell Miss Phillips. She didn't manage that until after dessert. Then she said, "Max...is...staying here."

"Oh?" The old lady lifted her nose and looked hard at Hannah.

Hannah didn't blush or look away. She just sat there. Her nose was red, her eyes full of tears, her sunshine hair droopy, and she returned Miss Phillips's long stare.

It was after eleven when Max crawled into her bed. She roused as he gathered her to him. She put a hand to his scratchy cheek and said, "Hello, darling."

He said chattily, "Amanda's home?"

"It surprised me, too," she whispered.

"You'll have to start controlling your shrieks of passion."

"I feel like a kept woman."

"No, no." He corrected her cheerfully. "It's your house. I'm a kept man."

He began to kiss down her chest, and that was shockingly erotic because his hot soft mouth and his scorching wet tongue were in such sharp contrast to his scratchy beard.

And he complained, "Why are you dressed?"

"Well, it seemed so *abandoned* to…get ready for you."

"Are you ready for me?" His voice was pleased.

"No, you sex maniac. I said I *didn't* get ready for you."

"Oh yes." His voice was a breeze of heat. "Oh, yes, you are."

Hannah cleaned the house for the next two days. It was as if she expected Mrs. Simmons to white-glove every baseboard, every light fixture. She exhausted herself. And then Max brought Geo two kittens. Two. Well, for Max that was probably restraint. Geo was highly entertained.

The kittens were little. Their eyes and ears were enormous, their bellies round, their legs short and their tails spiked. Geo chortled. The kittens taught Geo to treat them carefully. Max showed him how to hold the cats, and Geo lugged them everywhere. They would try to lick themselves or scratch, and they'd fall over and forget where they were. They were filled with curiosity, and were always underfoot.

Hannah told Max, "When you move out, Officer Simmons, the cats go with you."

But he only looked cocky as he said, "You've got me for life, Hannah Calhoun. Adjust."

She held him, and kissed him back, and wished to God she did have him for life.

The morning of the day his mother and his aunt were due to arrive, Hannah was up at five-thirty. Max asked sleepily, "You okay?"

Tersely, she replied, "Yes."

"What the *hell* are we doing up at this time of night?"

"It's daylight."

"Hannah, honey, it's only five-thirty!"

"There's a lot to do."

"How? Why?"

"Your mother's coming today."

He sat up and looked at her in surprise. "Hannah, she isn't going to *grade* you. You've already passed all the tests. You please *me*!"

All that proved was that he knew absolutely nothing about mothers. How could any man be twenty-eight years old, have had the same mother all that time, and know so little? It showed a basic flaw. Hannah gave Max a cool, surveying look. If he was that stupid about mothers, he could have other flaws as well. Of course! There was that purple room. She should have been warned.

"Are you sure we have to get up now?" he asked in a complaining way.

"You don't. Just me."

"What are you going to do?"

"I have to pick the flowers, and make the cookies. And straighten the house."

With a long sigh he lay back; then he heaved himself up and groused, "I'll help. It'll take half as long, then we can get at least another hour's sleep."

"If she breaks a cookie in half and looks at it critically, I'll pour the tea over her hat."

The laugh started in his throat and then spread to his stomach. He earnestly tried to control it, but it was hopeless from the start.

Hannah left the room. She put on scruffy jeans and a T-shirt. By seven-fifteen, she was finished with everything and had redone everything he'd done. She prowled through the house, twitching things and patting things and trying to think of exactly how she was going to tell Mrs. Simmons she really wasn't going to marry her son.

But she wanted Mrs. Simmons to see what a good housekeeper and cook she was, and what a beautiful child Geo was, so there would always be a kernel of regret in Max's mother's chest. It was a petty desire. She ought to be ashamed of such an unworthy longing, but she tried harder to make everything perfect. She went to the front door and looked at her house with a stranger's eyes.

It was beautiful. It was poor. It was sparse. The flowers were homegrown and plain. How

could flowers be plain? They were like homemade clothing. No, clothing could be done at
home and look handmade, not homemade. Who
could ever think of a flower as anything but
lovely? They were lovely, and there was that
jewel of a Phillips rug.

She spent the day developing a really impressive tension headache. She could devote the day
to that, because everything else that could possibly be done had all been done. She'd even
washed her car and vacuumed its inside.

She warned Max, "If by any chance they
should be here when you come home, don't you
call me Jewel Girl, or Baby Doll, or Snookums,
or..."

"I've never called you Snookums."

"And don't you dare do it when your mother's here."

"Okay, I'll call you Miss Calhoun." He was
enjoying himself.

She wasn't distracted. She said, "You call me
Hannah."

"I appreciate that."

He left for work at two-thirty, and Hannah
had only another endless hour and a half before
his mother arrived. His mother and his aunt. After lunch, Miss Phillips had said she was going

to her room. That was good. Hannah could face the Simmons women alone.

Geo got up from his nap, and she dressed him in a T-shirt and shorts. She'd had to resist buying him an asinine little-boy suit. She dressed in a pale gray summer cotton. It had a white collar and looked a little Pilgrimish. She didn't add a scarlet *A*.

They came almost as if they'd sat in the car for five minutes so they'd arrive right on the dot. They were nice women. Polite. They smiled and complimented her on the flowers and on the house, and agreed the facing on the fireplace was probably walnut.

They ate their cookies with relish and drank the tea without once mentioning Max or the possibility of a disastrous marriage between him and Hannah. Geo showed them the kittens, and they were very sweet about him.

...And Miss Phillips came down the stairs. She was dressed in a high-necked black handkerchief linen that had obviously cost more than Hannah made in a month. In the back of her hair she wore a high antique tortoiseshell comb. There were long pearl drop earrings in her wrinkled lobes, and the clasp at her throat was a cluster of marvelously luminous pearls. The rings on her fingers would have funded a small country.

Hannah gave her a careful look and introduced the guests to the old lady.

With her usual reserve, Miss Phillips seated herself, accepted a cup of tea, broke one of the cookies in two and frowned at it critically. She said, "I am Hannah's godmother."

That did surprise Hannah. At first she only thought what a sour fairy godmother; then she thought of the old woman coming down to give her consequence, to back her, and she was so touched.

Miss Phillips pierced the two visitors with her killing hawk stare and asked succinctly, "And what is your silly Aunt Ceilly doing these days?" She knew that would take them down a notch or two.

With droll Max-type humor, Mrs. Simmons replied, "Just about what you might expect. I was commissioned to give you a kiss from her."

Miss Phillips looked appalled. "Consider it done."

Mrs. Simmons laughed out loud. She reached into her purse and withdrew a letter. "And I was instructed to give you this. It might not make good sense."

Miss Phillips assured Mrs. Simmons, "Ceilly never did."

Again Mrs. Simmons laughed, and Hannah

began to regret that she would never be her daughter-in-law.

Then Max arrived! He came up on the front porch, whistling as if God was in His heaven and all was right with Max's world. But...he *didn't* use his key, so he still had some smarts. He rapped and waited. Geo ran shrieking a welcome, and Hannah opened the door to hiss under her breath, "What are you doing here?"

He kissed her startled mouth. "Hello there, Miss Calhoun." He removed his police cap and walked past her to greet his mother, his aunt and Miss Phillips, kissing each lady on the cheek. There is nothing more insidious than a charming man. *Then* he put an arm around Hannah in possessive smugness and asked, "How do you like my bride?"

"Max..." Hannah was appalled.

The three ladies beamed, and Max reached for Geo, picked him up and stood very smugly. "How do we look?" What could they say? Under those circumstances, how could they say anything?

Hannah's headache became blinding. Then Max's mother said, "He's told us all along that he was going to marry you. Right after they caught that Turner man the first time, he sent us the picture in the paper and said, 'This is the one.' We've all been so anxious he'd manage to snare you somehow."

Hannah was stunned. In a choking voice, she asked, "Didn't he tell you about...me? About Geo?"

"Oh, yes. Geo was in the newspaper picture, too. And Max told us the circumstances." She gave Hannah a kind, telling look. Then she added, "All of it."

Finally, Hannah said what was needed. "We really can't marry. It would ruin Max if this was used against him. He would have to spend his time defending me. He could never run for office, and our country needs him."

Max just smiled, and his mother was the one who said, "There are all sorts of ways to serve in public life. Max has made his choice. I'm just glad for him that you love him. He admires you tremendously. He brags about you so nicely."

Miss Phillips inquired in her abrupt way, "How did such a sensible family produce Ceilly?" And she frowned at them indignantly.

"We think a coo-coo bird tricked us."

And Miss Phillips laughed out loud. Hannah's heart overflowed with love, love for Miss Phillips, for Max's family, who intended to accept her, and for Max.

* * *

That night as they lay in bed, after Max had cured the dregs of her headache, she said, "I was going to give you up."

"You make me sound like a drug."

"Oh, Max, you *are*. Such an addictive one. I thought I'd ruin your whole life."

"You could only do that if you didn't marry me. Live with me and be my love." He was sleepy, and he settled her in his arms, with a strong indication that she should shut up and go to sleep.

Chattily she asked, "Can you imagine Miss Phillips coming down that way with all her war jewelry on and claiming to be my godmother?"

"Amanda is one of the earth's salts."

"And then *you* showing up!"

"I like my family, I wanted to say hello. Good night, Hannah."

"Think how Miss Phillips has changed!" He didn't reply, but she wasn't paying any attention. Then she said softly, "If Miss Phillips could change that much, maybe my family can."

"Maybe." He hugged her. "Hannah, you're a very special woman. We'll go see your family and set them straight."

Her eyes widened at the thought of Max "straightening out" her parents in his non-intrusive way. He probably could! "I love you,

Max. I don't think I can stand being this happy.''

"Are you?''

"Oh, Max.''

"Good. Go to sleep.''

* * * * * *